WITCH
ON THE WATER

Taste the Darkness!

ROWAN OF THE WOOD: BOOK TWO

WITCH
ON THE WATER

by Christine and Ethan Rose

BLUE
MOOSE
PRESS

Blue Moose Press
A division of Blue Moose Films, LLC
Austin, TX - *www.bluemoosefilms.com*

Copyright 2009 by Christine and Ethan Rose. All rights reserved.
Cover Design and Illustrations by Ia Ensterä, Wink Studios
Edited by Linda Thune
"Rowan Forlorn" Plate (page 13) by Geahk Burchill

ISBN-13: 978-0-9819949-2-5
First Edition.

ATTENTION ORGANIZATIONS AND SCHOOLS:
Quantity discounts are available on bulk purchases of this book for educational purposes or fund raising.

For information, go to *www.christineandethanrose.com*
www.rowanofthewood.com * *www.witchonthewater.com*

Library of Congress Control Number: 2009906913
Rose, Christine, 1969 -
  Rowan of the Wood / by Christine and Ethan Rose.
1. Wizards--Fiction. I. Rose, Ethan, 1968- II. Title.
ISBN-13: 978-0-9819949-2-5

Printed in the United States of America

For Ralph Pease, my mentor and friend

Thig an nathair as an toll

La donn Bride,

Ged robh tri traighean dh' an t-sneachd

Air leachd an lair.

"The serpent will come from the hole

On the brown Day of Bride,

Though there should be three feet of snow

On the flat surface of the ground."

—Author Unknown

THE MYTH

In th' mists of time of ages past,
Two mighty Druids were wed.
By truth and wisdom, strong and kind,
Their people would be led.

But raiders came from 'cross the sea
And tore the two asunder.
With blades of steel and a righteous god,
They came to kill and plunder.

The Samhain gate let some escape
And hide in the Summer Land.
Fiana went through; but Rowan remained
To protect their tribal band.

He waited too long; the door was gone
When he went to join his wife.
The men approached; he hid in his wand
To try and save his life.

In one year's time, the door would op'n,
Then Fiana could release him,
But a warrior monk then grabbed the wand
And carried it off on a whim.

When she returned, her heart did break.
Her love was not t'be found.
She vowed her life to find her love
And searched the world around.

She traveled far to tell her tale
With spells both canny n'strong.
The wand still lost, eluded by fate:
Her powers almost gone.

To another she went and power he lent
To keep her hale much longer.
A boon he sought; companions he gave
To continue her quest far stronger.

With th' Sons of Fey in canine form
And a century more of life,
She sought the spor though the trail was cold:
A true and faithful wife.

An impossible quest, pursued without rest,
But still she would not falter.
She searched the East; she searched the West.
Her goal she would not alter.

Her companions true, in closeness drew
And helped her on her way.
Sharing her road their pleasures few
Beside her never to stray.

Though th' road was dark; their future stark,
Their quest now grown to myth,
She journeyed on and left a cairn
For Rowan, a stone kiss.

New century gone and death approached.
A choice now had to be made.
To darkness turn and companions lose:
A grim and costly trade.

Moroi had come with their midnight ways
To offer life eternal.
Death the price and endless thirst,
Her fate now infernal.

The sun was lost; the earth was gained.
The canine spells were broken.
Two fled in fear; the mad remained.
Their bond now but a token.

Her soul was lost beyond recall.
Her quest became a danger.
If ever she found her missing love,
To him she'd be a stranger.

With darkness entwined; her power combined,
Would give rise to something evil.
Deep, dark despair would cover the earth
And cause a great upheaval.

So Arthur knew, and Duncan too,
That she could not succeed.
The Sons of Fey must find the wand,
So it could be concealed.

They traveled far on separate roads
'Til their quest had ended.
Now hidden deep 'neath puissant spells,
The wand, it fin'ly rested.

CHAPTER ONE

Circa 1422 A. D., London, England. In a cathedral, surrounded by a mob transfixed with reverential awe, Fiana stood staring at another disappointment. On the dais before her, a bishop, chanting in Latin, held up a fragment of wood.

It was not the one she was searching for.

She wove her way through the unwashed throng towards the exit.

As she turned onto the cold, darkened London streets, failure weighed down what was left of her fractured soul. She had been searching for centuries, but she found only dead ends. She had recently returned to the island where her homeland lay to the far north for the first time since she left it over eight hundred years ago. Needless to say, it had changed.

The world had changed, and so had she. The one thing that remained constant in her life was her quest for her imprisoned husband. Rowan was still in that wand somewhere, and she wouldn't stop looking until she found it. After all, she had given up her life for this. She wanted to stop, to rest, to be at peace, but there would be no peace until Rowan was released. She had lain this geas upon herself, and now she was trapped by it.

Fiana stopped, suddenly overwhelmed by the truth of it. Every so often, her age would become too real for her to handle. Although she still looked forty, she was nearly nine hundred. She had spent most of that time as a creature of the night, as they say. It had been the only way to remain "alive" and continue her quest. Her own magic had failed her after a short two hundred years. She had no choice. Become a moroi or give up and die.

Perhaps she should've given up.

Leaning against a stone wall for support, Fiana wiped her mouth with a cold, pale hand, trying to erase the dryness from her lips. The thirst. But there was only one thing that would quench her thirst. Blood. She hadn't fed in nearly two weeks, so she was weak. She always tried to go as long without blood as she could stand it. She didn't like having to scare people or hurt them. Still, her powers enabled her to make them forget most of the time. She held them spellbound when she could, suspending memory altogether, but if they resisted too much, then the traumatic memory couldn't be erased completely. In those instances, she did her best to alter the memory into something more pleasant. The entire thing was exhausting. She had been living—well, existing—like this for seven hundred years.

She wanted to stop all of it. Despair had overcome her, and she couldn't even think about what to do next. She needed some time alone, some time to herself, some time to gather the strength she would need to continue her hopeless quest.

She needed to feed.

Gathering up her will, she trudged on. Perhaps she would come across a creature more pathetic than she.

She really needed to feed.

Her thoughts wandered back to the wand and her beloved Rowan. She no longer had a trail to follow. Any trail there had been was lost in time and false leads. For now she was reduced to tracking down any and all bits of wood reputed to have magical properties. This had taken her across Asia and down into India and the Middle East. It was while there that she caught wind of a story called The Golden Legend, written by a bishop about a century ago. This legend stated that the origins of the True Cross predated Christ and even Judaism. It all started with a tree that grew up out of Adam's corpse. The Tree of Life, of course, for he was buried with a seed in his mouth.

She was not unfamiliar with the Tree of Life. It was tattooed on Rowan's chest and quite prevalent in their own mythos. It symbolized the cycle of life with its branches intertwining with its roots, but the Christian version of Tree of Life was quite different.

Going over their legend in her mind always brightened her spirits. It was just so absurd.

This new Tree of Life that grew out of Adam's grave was eventually chopped down and made into a bridge, over which the Queen of Sheba once crossed. She felt the power of the former tree and fell to the ground, worshipping it. She told King Soloman about the bridge and said that it would bring about the destruction of his people. Fearing that, Soloman had the bridge torn down and buried. It remained buried until some Roman soldiers happened upon it and built a crucifix out of it. Yes. The very same crucifix upon which their Christ was nailed.

Fiana laughed to herself.

"What people will believe," she said to the night.

She understood how legends work and shift and change. She had seen her husband's story go from the wizard trapped in the wand to being the man in the tree. After just a short century, Rowan and the Green Man were synonymous in many circles. Some had even merged them both with Cernunnos.

Such is the stuff of legends and myths. They grow and change, being what the people need them to be. Christian myths were no different. The Christian Church in Rome had become dangerously powerful across all of Europe and into the British Isles. Even her homeland of Caledonia, which they now called Scotland, had been overcome by it. She had watched the followers of this religion go from arrogant thugs, beating and torturing people who didn't believe, to hordes of people worshipping the supposed bones of the saints and the splinters of charlatans.

She even visited a church that claimed to have the brain of St. Peter.

Her task was not made any easier by the tendency for every Christian church or monastery to claim possession of a piece of the True Cross. Even the merchants along the streets hawked these relics, shouting into the streets stories of the miracles each had performed. The teeth of John the Baptist. The milk of the Virgin Mother. Back in Europe, the monks of Charroux had even claimed to have Christ's foreskin! All fake. People will truly believe anything to make their lives more bearable.

Fiana understood. For she still believed, after all these centuries, that she would find Rowan. It made her existence bearable.

For nearly two decades now she had been searching out these fragments and rejecting them one by one. Having seen so many of them, probably more than any Christian had, she was surprised both by how many of them came from different species of trees, and also how many came from what she could tell was the same tree. Whether or not their human god was killed on it, she could not tell. She did detect blood on some of them, but not always from the same person.

Not that she thought it mattered. To her all wood and indeed everything in the world was a divine creation, not only touched by divinity, but an integral part of it. She realized that what the Christians called "God" was the oneness of everything. To her, everyone and everything was a part of "God." Therefore every piece of wood she saw, whether revered or not, was magical in some way. But none of them were the particular piece of a rowan tree that held her long lost husband.

She felt lost, too. Lost and alone. No longer a part of the world. She needed to find some forest lands to reconnect and heal her shattered spirit. Tears of frustration dampened her face.

This city would not end. She continued walking down its ever-winding narrow streets, bracing herself against the autumn wind. The stench in this city was almost intolerable. Filth and urine and feces and other horrid smells filled every alleyway she passed. Pigs, tethered to homes and businesses, rolled in the muck thrown out of household windows. Those pigs would make a nice blood meal, and she was so hungry. But they do have a tendency to squeal. She certainly didn't need an angry mob on her tail, so she would have to wait a little longer to eat.

The curfew bell rung out from various places around the city. She picked up her pace.

Up ahead in the darkness, she could just make out the Boar's Head sign hanging above a door. Finally, the Inn where Moody waited for her. She felt something close to panic at the thought of facing the crowd of people who were sure to be filling the common room. The entire city was in mourning over the recent loss of their King Henry V. And they were all buzzing about the new king, an infant. She didn't want to listen to drunken toasts to the the former king and theories about what would happen to the country in the hands of Gloucester and Bedford until the infant king came of age. What she needed was solitude. So she slipped into the crude lean-to which served as a stable. The only inhabitants she could see were a pair of oxen.

Food, she thought. She held her breath and listened intently to her surrounding, making sure she was indeed alone. She heard some snuffling sobs issuing from the straw pile. So she wasn't the first to come here for a good cry. Somehow, knowing someone else was in pain made it easier to deal with her own. Helping others pushed her own misery into the background.

"Come out of there lass," she said gently. "Tell me your troubles, and we will see what can be done."

The snuffling stopped abruptly as if breath was being held.

Fiana waited patiently.

After a moment, the dirty, tear-streaked face of a scullery maid peeked out from behind the straw to examine her. Fiana submitted to the examination with poise.

"Who are you?" the girl finally asked.

"Someone seeking respite from her own despair by listening to the troubles of others. Come, tell me your tales of woe, and we will see if there is aught I can do for you."

The girl of about thirteen or fourteen years emerged hesitantly, then looked down at her dirty feet sadly. She wore nothing more than rags for clothes, but beneath the dirt, Fiana could see that she was comely.

Fiana waited for the confession, but none came. The girl just stood awkwardly with her head bowed and her hands clasped tightly together.

"Do you work here?" asked Fiana to get her started.

The girl nodded mutely then looked up with sudden defiance. She finally spoke, and it all came out angrily at once. "It is my Inn. My father left it to me. His brother runs it now that he's dead. He was my guardian before I came of age, but now he's going to force me to marry him so he can get ownership."

"Surely the relationship is too close for a legal marriage," Fiana said.

"He bought a dispensation from the bishop. Now I have no choice."

"There is always a choice. Let us put our minds to the task and see what we can come up with. What is your name?"

"Sara," the girl said.

"Well, Sara. I am Fiana. Come, sit near me and we shall think of something."

Inside, the tap room was quite busy. Patrons who had traveled far to see the fragment of the True Cross within the cathedral crowded the benches. But now that their holy duty was done they wanted to relax with a pint of weak beer.

The tapster was in a foul mood. Normally, he would be pleased at the full room since it had a sympathetic effect on his coffers, but the disappearance of his niece left him without a serving maid. He was himself nearly forty and of substantial girth. All this running back and forth with trays of beer was hard on his knees. Finally, exasperated beyond endurance, he called Molly from the scullery to take over for him while he went to look for Sara.

When he stepped forth into the cool night to look around, he beheld a beautiful woman with flowing red locks sitting on the edge of his well, idly playing with a polished stick, almost as if praying a rosary. Sara sat beside her.

"Get yer tail inside, you ingrate. There's work to be done," Thomas shouted.

Sara stood up with her head bowed low. The woman touched her hand and smiled.

Sara lifted her head up high and strode past Thomas with a confidence that he had never seen.

But Thomas could not move. He stood transfixed by the beauty before him. She looked up at him with green eyes that invited him to come closer. He did without hesitation. She stopped him at arms length with the strange polished stick, but he didn't care. He couldn't stop looking into her eyes. Those magnificent green eyes.

"This is a very pleasant spot," she said. "But a little too exposed. What it really needs is a tree to shade and protect it." She pushed the stick into his belly, slightly denting the fat and letting him know she meant business. "Just like your niece Sara needs someone to protect her. Would you do that for me?"

Thomas tried to open his mouth and let her know that he would do anything she desired of him, but was unable to. She seemed to hear him anyway, for she nodded and smiled.

"That is good," she said getting to her feet and slipping the polished wood into her sleeve as she walked past him and into the stable. He tried to follow but his roots had sunk too far into the earth. He was as immovable as the tree he had become.

Later, Sara fetched a cup of red wine for Fiana and a pint for her jolly companion. They toasted to Sara's good fortune and success.

Back in the stable, the oxen used their tails to brush flies away from the fresh puncture wounds on their necks.

CHAPTER TWO

Cullen sneezed. Grappling for a Kleenex beside his bed, he heard Rex's snores falter. He froze and held his breath. Rex turned over and started to snore again. Cullen slowly and quietly took the last Kleenex from the box. He blew his nose, covering his head with the comforter to mute the sound. He tossed the used tissue to the floor in the pile with the others.

Must pick those up before they wake up, he thought.

He groaned into the underside of his blanket. Even his groan was nasally. He hated being sick. It didn't make things better knowing Trudy would think he was faking it. He would've given anything to stay in bed all day and read. Of course, the only book he had at home was his History text, but that would do just fine. After all, history is just a collection of stories, a Cliff Notes version. Cullen filled in the rest with his imagination.

Rex rolled over above him again.

He sure is restless this morning, Cullen thought, then groggily contemplated getting up. He didn't want to be in the room when Rex woke up. Sometimes he made Cullen literally kiss his feet as a morning ritual. If Cullen refused, he got punched in the nose. It's better all around to just avoid the entire business.

But Cullen didn't get up yet. He chanced a few more moments bundled under his Batman comforter. He remembered having the strangest dream. He was at school in the hallway and thirsty. Really thirsty. He stooped over the water fountain to get a drink. He felt cold wetness hitting his face, but he couldn't get it in his mouth. His tongue lolled out and around, but never touched the water. It felt like a cotton ball, and no matter how far he stuck it out he couldn't get it wet. What a nightmare!

Cullen sneezed. Groan.

As if his head wasn't full enough with a heart-broken, brooding wizard trapped inside. Now it was doubly full with sickly mucus. *Where did it all come from? My head isn't that big!* he thought as he looked at the pile of used tissues next to his bed.

Rex's snores faltered again.

Okay. Getting up.

He needed some water, even if it wouldn't get rid of the awful taste in his mouth. He reached for the last piece of his solitary Christmas candy hidden under his mattress. Sugar would help cut that taste.

Rowan had been very quiet over the past six weeks. Sometimes Cullen almost forgot he was there. But he still felt the heaviness of the wizard's grief, even though he knew Rowan was blocking the bulk of it. He hadn't thought a word to Cullen since Fiana escaped from the redwoods last November. They hadn't talked in his dreams. He hadn't transformed. Nothing. Nothing at all in over six weeks. It was almost as if it had all been a strange dream. Almost. But one doesn't normally share dreams with one's teacher and friends. They remembered, too. He knew they'd want to talk about it—again. Women like to talk. He just wanted to put it behind him and move on. Perhaps Rowan would stay quiet and he'd eventually forget he was there.

After Cullen put the last of the used tissues in the wastebasket, he unwrapped the small piece of remaining candy cane and popped it into his mouth. The sugary goodness immediately cut through the sickly film.

He heard a toilet flush from Trudy's room, and a wave of panic rushed through him.

Grabbing his empty water glass, he rushed out.

With a little uncustomary luck, the coffee was actually ready by the time his foster mother entered the kitchen. He would have to prepare the grounds before bed more often. It's so easy to just flip a switch in the morning.

Trudy groaned, her way of saying "Good Morning! Thanks for the coffee!"

Cullen sat down at the table and took a sip of orange juice, wincing as the acidic drink washed across his bottom lip, split from the parched dream. It tasted funny, like he had just brushed his teeth, even though he hadn't. All his taste buds were muted and nothing could quench his thirst. He wondered if this is what it was like to be a vampire: an unquenchable thirst for all eternity. He had a brief moment of sympathy for Fiana.

Very brief.

Speaking of unquenchable thirst, he thought as he watched Trudy abandon her coffee and pour herself her morning drink. Her sunken eyes surveyed him with mistrust as she looked at him from over her martini glass, but she didn't say anything about his wan appearance.

"Ready to go back to school today?" she asked.

"Yes, ma'am."

"Even though your grounding officially ends this morning, I expect more from you than the ingratitude you showed us by running away."

"I didn't run away, I—"

"You ran away!" she said decisively, throwing her flattened palm up between them.

"Yes, ma'am." He really did know better than to argue.

"You're walking to school today I presume?" she said, then sipped her drink again. Her mood was already improving.

"Yes, ma'am—I mean, if that's okay." Best she thinks it's her idea.

"That's fine. It will keep me from having to take you. I'm feeling a little under the weather and so is Rex. We're staying home today." She took another sip. Cullen was not surprised to see that her drink was nearly gone.

"Thanks. I'll just go get ready so I won't be late." Even though he felt miserable, the thought of a day at school without Rex was a pleasant one.

"What about breakfast?"

"I'm not that hungry." It was true; his illness didn't leave him with much of an appetite.

"Not yours, mine!"

"Oh, of course," Cullen said back paddling, "What would you like?"

"Um, not eggs—too heavy. How about some oatmeal? It's supposed to have anti-oxidant properties or some such nonsense." Trudy settled herself at the table and finished her drink which was also chock full of antioxidants, being mostly vodka. Cullen didn't know how any cold germ survived!

Trudy rubbed her hands over her face and massaged her sunken eyes. "I feel like a truck hit me."

Cullen thought she looked like it, too.

He put a pot on to boil and rushed back to his room to get dressed. He nearly ran smack dab into Frank coming from his room.

"Watch it, boy," Frank said gruffly.

"Sorry sir. The water's on to boil for the oatmeal."

"Oatmeal! What happened to my bacon and eggs? Horse food is no way to start the day. I'm a man, dammit. I need my sustenance. I swear to God, that woman…" he grumbled as he continued towards the kitchen, knowing he would have to take it up with Trudy and her latest fad diet, none of which ever worked primarily because she figured since alcohol had "empty" calories, they didn't count.

Cullen ducked into his room and quietly got dressed. Rex still snored from the top bunk. By the time he got back to the kitchen, the water was at a perfect rolling boil, so he added the oats. Frank and Trudy were squabbling at the table about food. Frank was spouting stuff about the food chain again, and Trudy was talking about his health. If it was possible, Frank was even larger *after* being on a diet. Cullen figured it was because he cheated much more when he was away from home, with fast food and the like.

"Fine!" Trudy screamed. "You can have your bacon, but you have to have fakin' bacon today because we're out of regular bacon. Cullen, make some of that fakin' bacon in the microwave for your father."

He's not my father, Cullen thought at the exact same time that Frank said, "I'm not his father!"

"Stop being such a grouch, Frank. It's still fat and salt, just like real bacon—it's just vegetable fat instead of animal fat. You'll like it."

Frank mumbled to himself about how he doubted it, probably resolving to hate it no matter how good it tasted. He picked up the paper and snapped it erect between he and Trudy, determined to stop the conversation.

Trudy got up and made another drink.

After breakfast, Cullen bundled up extra warmly to keep out the cold. His scarf was wrapped tightly around his face so that only his glasses showed between it and his hat. They were already fogging up from the warm breath seeping upward from behind the scarf. He lifted a gloved hand and waved to Trudy and Frank, still squabbling at the table. They didn't see him go.

The air was clean and crisp; and, although he couldn't breathe out of his nose, he knew it smelled fresh. He felt the coolness penetrate his jeans and all three layers on top as he entered his beloved redwoods. No matter how much time he spent here, it always held the same mystical feeling of magic for him.

Rowan stirred in his head. This was the first time they had been in the forest since Fiana's escape. She had sucked all of Rowan's energy through a kiss and disappeared, leaving Rowan feeling betrayed and heartbroken. And if Rowan felt it, so did Cullen.

Cullen began to feel hot despite the cold air around him. He dared not take off anything, though. He would just have to deal with the sweat today, even if it did make his hair stand on end. At least Rex wouldn't be there. The ridicule might be kept to a minimum.

"Cullen?" Rowan spoke.

It had been so long, that Cullen thought it came from outside of him. He stopped in his tracks and looked around him. No one was there.

"Cullen. It is I, Rowan. I am inside you, remember?"

"How could I forget," Cullen said out loud sullenly and began walking again, shoving his hands deep into his pockets. "Where have you been?"

"Here. Always here."

"Yep, but you've been very quiet."

"Yes. I had much to think about and work through. I did not wish to burden you any more than I already have," Rowan said.

This was awkward. What did they really have to talk about? It was like having your father with you all the time. They had nothing in common except sharing Cullen's body and nearly being killed by a psychotic vampire.

"She is not psychotic," Rowan answered Cullen's thought.

"Perhaps you weren't in the same dungeon as I was being tortured by her, but trust me—she's psychotic." Cullen was angry, and it surprised him as much as it surprised Rowan.

"She is my wife, and she has had a very rough existence."

"Not as rough as her victims! She nearly killed me, Rowan, and she put my friends in danger. How do you expect me to feel? I can't believe you are defending her!" If anyone was around, they would think Cullen was the crazy one, yelling to himself in the middle of a redwood forest.

"She sacrificed her humanity for me. To find me. She has just lost her way."

"Rowan. She eats people."

"You are right, she is confused; but I know her essence."

"Yeah, yeah. I've heard it before. She's good deep down. Right?"

Cullen turned onto the road, the last part of his commute.

Rowan was quiet for a long time. Cullen was, too.

Cullen felt hurt and frustrated, and he knew Rowan could feel it, too. He didn't have the control to block his emotions the way Rowan did. Even if Cullen did have the strength, he wouldn't block them. *He should feel what I feel. It's my body!*

Rowan remained quiet, probably mulling over possible things to say.

Cullen wouldn't listen to what he had to say anyway. It wouldn't change anything, so he just wallowed in all the circumstances and events which made his life a constant misery.

"You are unwell," Rowan said sympathetically.

"What tipped you off?" Cullen lashed out and then coughed, fogging up his glasses all over again. He didn't know where all this anger was coming from.

"I can barely hear you through the fog in your head."

"It's called a cold, Rowan. I have a cold," Cullen said as he turned onto the road which would lead him the rest of the way to school.

"Perhaps it is why you are so angry. You feel ill."

It probably did have something to do with his short temper this morning, but Cullen wouldn't admit it.

"Sure, that's it. It wouldn't have anything to do with nearly being tortured to death by your ex. I didn't ask for this. Any of it." Sweat poured down Cullen's face, soaking his cinched hoodie beneath the hat and scarf. He didn't care about being sick anymore. He ripped off his hat and threw back his hood. The cold air pleasantly stung his wet forehead, and he could feel the heat rise off the top of his head. It must look like his head was smoking to passersby in their cars.

Cullen coughed and sniffled.

"*Slàinte*," Rowan said from inside Cullen's head, and suddenly his cold was gone. Just like that. He breathed in the cold air deeply through his newly cleared nostrils. It hurt his nose and his lungs, but he could breathe again.

"Thanks," Cullen said hesitantly. He felt so much better. Magic was pretty cool, he guessed. It wasn't all bad having an ancient wizard trapped inside him. There were little perks, but he wasn't sure they were worth the danger.

"So, you can do magic to me while you're inside me, but can you do magic through me?" Cullen perked up thinking that he could maybe do magic, or at least appear to do magic. His life would be so much easier with that kind of power. He was almost to school, and he could already hear the kids milling about as they got off the buses up ahead. He daydreamed about turning certain football players into frogs, namely Scott, Fred, Todd, and especially Rex, the next time they tormented him.

"Magic is not to be used for convenience, Cullen. Responsibility comes with such power, and I feel responsible for you and your well being."

The anger welled up inside Cullen again.

Not to be used for convenience, huh? Or at least only to be used for your own convenience and no one else's, Cullen thought fiercely to Rowan. They were too close to school now for him to be talking aloud to apparently no one. He certainly didn't need to give the other kids any more reason to taunt him.

"It is not to be used for any convenience or abused. I helped you feel better as a peace offering. We must live together in here. We have no choice."

Look, I'm at school now, so I would appreciate you keeping quiet in there and not distracting me. We can talk about this later.

Cullen ended the conversation.

He marched up the steps and went into homeroom.

CHAPTER THREE

Northern California, 1860 A. D. Wesh-et-wah looked down at his blood-stained hands as he swept through the forest with his eight-year-old son. It was her blood. Their blood. The tears burning in his eyes did not cool his grief nor did they stay his stride. He needed to get away. Save his son. Disappear into the mist-haunted depths of the redwood forest. He would go to the southern Tehwon village, and together they'd seek out the Winnau people, a nearby tribe who had thus far been spared the white man's wrath. They lived deep in the woods to the southeast. If he moved closer to them, perhaps he could keep his son safe.

Reaching the end of his emotional strength, Wesh-et-wah stopped, sank down into the lush ferns, and wept. Tiny hands patted his shoulder. With tear-filled eyes, he looked up at his son. His son was too young to know such tragedy. The image of his son, blurred through his tears, standing before him was his only reason to go on living. But he couldn't shake the image of his wife and daughter lying there in their own blood amongst the rest of their tribe. They had been all huddled together as if protecting each other from a force against which there was no protection.

The harmony of existence was broken. A rip had been torn in the reality of his universe and through it poured a disruptive evil.

There had always been tribal differences and even disagreements within his own tribe, but there had also always been respect. These newcomers, pale as death, had none. Not for the native peoples. Not for the Earth and all Her gifts. Not even for each other. The carnage in which they reveled was beyond belief.

Only yesterday, he had been hunting with his son. It had been a great time to be a father: a time to pass on his knowledge of the world. Wesh-et-wah had been teaching his son the art of tracking deer. It was customary on the night before their annual Circle of Life celebration for the men to gather supplies and remain out overnight with their sons, teaching them the ways and customs of their people. The the wives and daughters stayed behind to prepare for the great celebration. When the men returned with fresh meat, fish, and other supplies, the entire tribe would eat and dance and sing.

There would be no singing today.

His feet would never dance again, for they danced because of her.

And now, she was gone.

The nausea in his body made ever eating again unthinkable. All that blood. All their blood.

He and his son had returned with a fresh deer for the feast, but all was silent. No laughter came from children at play. No women talked amongst themselves as they worked. No one ran to greet them with praise for their hunting prowess.

No one had moved at all.

He had looked over the slaughtered remains of his tribe with disbelief. He had tried to make sense of the scene, but there was no reason to it. They had all just lain there in strange, twisted heaps.

Then he had heard the laughter. It was a harsh, foul sound bursting forth from the throats of evil men, like pus from a boil. The marauders, led by a man they called "The Thug," who was hated even by other white men, sat just off-shore in their boat and laughed. The Thug and the men with him held bloody hatchets, wooden clubs, and knives. They were all covered in the blood of his family and tribe.

Wesh-et-wah could not make sense of it. No rage came as the laughter went on. The white men rowed away toward the main land, and Wesh-et-wah stood over his dead wife, catatonic. All the sounds of life seemed to cease. He no longer heard the waves of the great water. He no longer heard the birds. He only heard the beating of his broken heart and his shallow breathing. Then from out of the tunneled silence, he heard a child cry. He looked up to see his chief, Sergeant Joe, holding his own infant son. His face was contorted in grief as he clutched the baby to his chest, kneeling beside his fallen wife.

Ten years ago the white men had started coming, and they had just kept coming. And coming. Greed brought them. Blood lust kept them. Their weapons were no match for his people. When these white men wanted something, they took it. It did not matter that they were unwelcome. They took the Tehwon women and left them used and bloodied, crying in shame. They forced the men to work, to find their yellow metal for them while they drank the fire water, which only made them more cruel.

Even through his grief and despair, he knew what must be done. He could not stay in this place of death. He could never return to Kalawi Island, this ruin which was once his home. His son was all he had left, and so he must keep him safe.

He got up out of the ferns and kept walking, his son following. There must be other survivors from his tribe looking for a
new place to live. Perhaps they, too, would go south to another
Tehwon village. Perhaps they would stay and fight the white
man and seek revenge for this massacre. Then they, too, would
die. For to fight the white man was suicide. Still, the thought
of death in battle, for honor, was attractive. At least this pain
would stop—this suffocating pain.

He shook off the thought. He must keep his son safe.

He thought again of the Winnau. They had protection from
the white man: a small powerful talisman. He had heard the
stories by the fire at night, but he thought it just superstition.
Until now.

Through the generations, from grandfather to father to
son, the Winnau had passed down this special piece of knotty
wood for protection. It is said, many generations ago, that their
people traded with some white fur traders far, far north, in the
land of the Enuiae. Alaska. These men had come from the west
and traded knives and needles for furs. Before continuing on
their journey, the trader men found a Winnau tribe in the Nuti
and tried to subjugate them through work and religion. They
claimed the Winnau land for their own and buried a bottle with
parchment and this knotty wood stuffed inside, promising they
would return to rule.

Soon after the white man left, however, the Winnau dug up
the bottle and smashed it against the rocks. They burned the
parchment but took the talisman, sensing the wholesome power
within it. They gave it to their shaman who verified the power.
After this they began a long southward migration in fear of the
white man's return, for they had heard stories of what these men
had done in the north. They only wanted to live in peace, and
peace was not possible with the white man.

Now generations later, it has made its way down far into Wesh-et-wah's own lands, in the forests of the red wood. It is said that anyone who has this knotty wood talisman knows when to leave before the white man can come. Some believe it even makes them invisible to the white man.

Wesh-et-wah decided he must get this sacred wood from the Winnau to protect his son and the remainder of his people. A massacre such as this could never happen again. Never, ever happen again.

He arrived in the southern Tehwon village late in the day with his story of mass murder. It was their custom not to speak of the dead. They would say, "Indian die, Indian not speak," but he could not keep himself quiet. He must talk of it or burst.

"There was so much blood," he began. The tears stung his eyes, and he tried to look away. His son held tightly to his arm, his face as ghostly as the white man's.

"I couldn't bring myself to do anything, and the white men just laughed at our grief. There was so much blood. They did not use their guns. They used hatchets and knives. Heads were cleaved in two, so many were unrecognizable."

He stopped and lowered his head.

The people of this village listened patiently with sorrow in their eyes, but showed no surprise.

"Yes, Wesh-et-wah. There were two other massacres last night. You are not the only Tehwon mourning today. Others have come here and to the village to the north for shelter and solace. They, too, want protection and revenge."

Everyone was quiet for a long time.

"Where is your shaman. I need a healing ceremony. I want her to remove the silak from me and stop this pain."

"She is resting. A disturbance during her monthly ritual made her very sick. She felt blood up on the mountaintop. The power gained during her sacred blood-time intensified the impact on her," the Tehwon chief said. "But, Wesh-et-wah, your pain cannot be removed like other silak. This pain you suffer must be used to remember the fallen and to remember the cruelty of the white man. We must not be caught so helpless again."

"I know a way to protect us from the white man's wrath and murder," Wesh-et-wah said, replacing his pain with anger. "There is a powerful talisman said to contain a forest spirit. The Winnau people to the east have it among them. It has protected them from the white man. I say it is our turn to be protected. We must have that talisman. I will not see my son or any more of my people hurt."

All eyes looked at their chief in unison.

"They will not give it freely," the Tehwon chief said quietly, "but I agree, we must be protected. There will be no bloodshed. Enough blood has been spilled. We must obtain it secretly."

"I have seen where they keep it," a young boy spoke up. "I was out with my father hunting, and we met with some Winnau people. They invited us back and showed us their village. It was supposed to be secret, but a boy showed me the talisman and told me of its powers of protection."

"Tell us more, boy. Where is it kept?" the chief demanded.

"All their houses are round like ours, but there is one that is like a small tee-pee. Inside they sweat and pray. They keep the talisman there inside a wooden box carved with the leafy face of an old man," the boy replied.

"A leafy face?" the chief asked.

"Yes. The forest spirit inside the talisman is an old, powerful magic man, they say. The box was carved long ago to honor his sacrifice. It is his power that protects them from the white man."

There was murmuring amongst the tribe, but the chief raised a hand and they all became silent.

"We will get this wand to protect us, but not tonight. We must plan and gather more information. The weary must rest. The hungry must eat.

"Ken-na-wah, get some food for our guests," he said to his wife. "Tonight we will plan. Tomorrow we will act."

The tribe turned to their neighbors around the fire and began talking amongst themselves. Ken-na-wah brought some acorn mash, oysters, and water to Wesh-et-wah and his son. Wesh-et-wah accepted the food gifts gratefully with a bow of his head. He saw that Ken-na-wah's moccasins were embroidered with the rose flower. This had been his wife's name, and the nauseous grief returned with more tears. She tenderly touched his cheek before turning away. His eyes focused on the long leather strands dangling from her breast and arms, dancing in the light breeze, hypnotizing him into comfortable catatonia.

His son ate, but Wesh-et-wah had no appetite for food or drink. His thoughts were on the talisman as he stared out into the dark distance, beyond the fire. There a shape began to take form. It was a white man in the shadows, bound and gagged. Wesh-et-wah jumped up, spilling the food from his lap, and rushed over to the white man with his knife drawn. It was already against the white man's throat when the chief spoke.

"No, Wesh-et-wah. He is not our enemy."

Wesh-et-wah looked up toward the fire, and saw the silhouette of the chief's ornate headdress against the orange glow.

"He is a white man. They are all our enemies."

"Not this one. He has come with those from Nova Scotia, not for the yellow stones. He also has interest in this talisman you speak of. He had agreed to earn our trust before we discuss anything further. He knows what men of his color have done to us."

Wesh-et-wah stepped back, roughly pushing the bound man aside, and walked back toward the fire.

"Rest for tonight. We will seek our protection tomorrow," the chief said.

Ken-na-wah showed Wesh-et-wah and his son to a place to sleep. His mind was silent for a short time, despite the faint sound of a steady rattle and the mournful cry of the love flute. Finally, sleep overtook Wesh-et-wah.

Weeks passed. They sent scouts out every night to spy on the Winnau tribe, learning more about their ways and their plans. Finally, the time came when they thought they could risk stealing the talisman. It was during a fertility celebration for the young women of the tribe. The men would be away with their sons. The Winnau were known for their hunting skills. They hunted deer by running them down, so they knew they couldn't outrun the Winnau men. The Tehwon scouts had to be very careful, for if they were caught they could not get away.

Wesh-et-wah was among those who went to get the talisman, as it was his idea, and he was one of the stealthiest of the tribe. They crouched behind the trees nearby and watched as the ceremony took place. The elder women began to tattoo the adolescent girls' noses, cheeks, and chins with tribal designs, a sign of womanhood in their village.

Wesh-et-wah couldn't help but see the correlation between what they were doing to these peaceful people and what the white men had done to his own village. They were acting when the village was the most vulnerable. But no blood would be shed tonight. The Winnau women were distracted by their celebration, and no one was near the sacred tent.

The Tehwon men crouched low as they approached the round houses, making sure they stayed out of sight. They had a good plan. One man on the opposite side of the sacred tent made a loud but natural noise, like a branch breaking. All the women and girls looked that way simultaneously, and Wesh-et-wah slipped into the sacred tent. It was empty except for some stones, a flat drum decorated with a black and red deer that hung on the wall, a carved out stone full of water, and the carved wooden box. Just as the boy had said, the box looked like an old man with a long beard entangled with leaves. Its eyes were wide with wonder and its mouth open in joy. Carved leaves surrounded the face and were actually painted green. It was a beautiful box, but his instructions were clear. Take the talisman. Leave the box. They hoped the Winnau would not miss the talisman for many days or weeks because the box would still be there.

Wesh-et-wah held his breath and opened the box. Inside was a knotty piece of wood, natural, not carved. It looked just like a normal piece of wood, something that you would just walk right by if you saw it lying on the ground, only polished. It was obviously very old and rather longer than he had expected. He picked it up and immediately felt the powerful energy emanating from it. This was certainly the talisman that would help his people. He tucked it inside his belt, put the box back exactly like it was, and waited for the second distraction to leave. It came, this time a rustling in the ferns. The women stopped again and looked toward the sound. All Indians were on edge with the white man so near. Even natural sounds caused pause.

Wesh-et-wah slipped out as stealthily as he had come in.

Before the Tehwons even left the area, they heard the screams. Peering back through the trees, Wesh-et-wah and the others witnessed the white man's vicious decimation of the Winnau women.

Their savage brutality had no limits.

Ruthless images surpassed Wesh-et-wah's comprehension, burned forever in his mind. He had no words for what the white men did, and they sadistically smiled while they did it. Splattered with the blood of the Winnau women, the white men laughed loudly and crowed into the night.

The slaughter was over as quickly as it had began. The screams replaced with laughter, and then silence. The white men had wasted no time.

Wesh-et-wah couldn't help but think it was his fault. He had taken their protection away. It couldn't be a coincidence that the attack occurred right after the talisman left the village.

CHAPTER FOUR

Max MacFey sat at her kitchen table with a bowl of fruit and a glass of water. Shadow, her cat, walked across the table in front of her and helped herself to some water from Max's glass. She liked to walk on the table, literally right under Max's nose, sometimes flicking it with the end of her fuzzy tail because she knew that Max would pick her up and cradle her in the crook of one arm where she would rest with her eyes half closed, purring contently, until it no longer pleased her to be there. Max did just that and put her nose right up to the cat's teeny-tiny nose and said, "Good morning, my sweet."

Max was very glad school was starting today. Too often she had sat alone at a restaurant waiting for her food over the holidays. She wanted to do something special and get out, but it didn't really make the holidays any less lonely. Eating alone at a fancy restaurant perhaps felt even lonelier than eating alone at home. This year felt even more lonesome than the previous ones, for she could still feel his strong hands helping her up. His touch on her arm had awoken something inside her that had been sleeping for too long. She missed her family, but she hadn't really missed romance. There were more important things after all. Career, for one. But now she couldn't remember all the other reasons she had steered clear of it. It had to be more than just career, right? Now, of course, she only wanted him. A fourteen-hundred-year-old wizard. Ridiculous. It wasn't just his age—he lived inside a boy! Thinking about Rowan romantically just didn't seem right. Even when he was in his own form, Cullen was still there somewhere inside.

It was just wrong on so many levels.

Shadow wiggled out of her arms and went to curl up in a dark corner somewhere. Max took the opportunity to put her to-go coffee mug in the microwave. It was almost time to leave, and it would be good to get back to work. She needed to go back to work. She needed the hallways full of chattering and screeching teens and tweens. She needed the distraction. And she needed the company.

After their return from that very strange night in San Francisco, she thought that Moody, her great-great-great-great-great-great-great fey uncle, would offer some familial company over the holidays; but he had mysteriously disappeared from Fortuna before Thanksgiving. He hadn't been heard from or seen since. He hadn't even said goodbye.

She put on her coat over her other three layers and remembered the snow and freezing cold at Christmastime with her family back east. Here in California it wasn't really freezing, and no snow. It wasn't warm enough for spring wear and not cold enough for winter wear. It forced her to dress in layers each day. It was colder in the mornings, so she dressed warmer and then peeled off layers as the day progressed. She missed the snow, she decided. She had a fireplace, and it was at least cold enough at night for that. *Small blessings*, she thought and smiled. But to share that roaring fire cuddled up with Rowan, in his strong arms…

"Stop it," she said aloud to herself. "I'm enjoying the gift that is now. I'm not dwelling on the past or the future. I'm enjoying the gift that is now." The affirmations helped sometimes. Only sometimes. Still, they were no substitution for a warm body and someone to love.

The microwave beeped, and it pulled her out of her daydream. Coffee ready. Off to school.

Elsewhere in Fortuna, Maddy meticulously put on her black eyeliner. She had turned thirteen the week following her San Francisco adventure last November, so she was allowed to wear make up now. She wore it before, of course, but she had to put it on at school and take it off before she got home. Now she could get ready at home. Her mother didn't like it much, but—fortunately for Maddy—she believed in self-expression. Being the hippie chick she was, her mother didn't wear any makeup, not even the natural stuff. She reluctantly agreed to let Maddy wear makeup, but it had to be natural and not tested on animals. Whatever. As if it really mattered anyway. She may only be thirteen, but she was smart enough to know that what people do doesn't really make any difference. Sure, as a species humans were destroying the planet, but what difference could a single person make?

She wore her jet black hair up in two high ponytails. Her mother wouldn't let her dread her hair. Whatever, again. That was natural! So she used a thin curling iron to make ringlets. When both eye's eyeliner were perfectly matched, she started applying the black eye shadow. She loved the way her bright green eyes seemed to jump out of her head when surrounded by black and framed by her black bangs, which hung above her eyebrows in a harsh, straight line. Dark purple lipstick was the finishing touch, and she looked great.

Ready for school—and just in time too.

"Maddy, April's here," her mother shouted from across the house.

"Madeline. My name is Madeline," she said under her breath. She looked at herself once more in the mirror and adjusted the arm warmers to ensure they hid all they were supposed to. These were her favorite pair. She got them for Christmas, or Solstice as her mother and Linda insisted on calling it. It really was celebrated the same way: presents, evergreen tree, wreaths, mistletoe. Maddy preferred it anyway, as it was one of the eight witch sabbats. Anyway, these arm warmers were so cool because they were black with white skeleton arms on the tops, so it looked like death was grabbing at your hands. They were so totally badass.

"Bye mom," she shouted as she opened the door and went out toward April's mother's car. She could see April's face through the back window, as if she was watching Maddy come down the walk. But Maddy knew April couldn't see her anymore.

"Don't forget your lunch," her mom said, appearing at the door with her lunch box. It was an old-school metal kind, shaped like a coffin with Jack Skelton on the front. She tossed it across the front yard to Maddy.

"Thanks," Maddy said catching it, and she got into the car with April and her mom.

"Remember, Linda and I are going to that Proposition 8 protest today," Maddy's mother shouted. Linda was Maddy's mother's wife—or husband. Life-partner. They had been married the year before, but now their marriage was said to be invalid by the state. It was a thing.

"We probably won't be back when you get home today, so I'll leave your dinner in the fridge."

Maddy sunk down in her seat. "Whatever," she mumbled. Maddy loved Linda, she was pretty cool; but Fortuna was still a relatively conservative town. She didn't have to shout it out for everyone to hear.

"Hey Carol," April's mother waved to Maddy's mom, who leaned against the doorway sipping her coffee. "Heading up to Arcata today?"

"Hi Joan," Maddy's mother said, waving back. "Yep. Campus rally. Hey, thanks for taking the girls."

"My pleasure. Give 'em hell!" Mrs. Burton said, holding a clenched fist up in solidarity, and then pulled forward away from Maddy's house.

Carol Wells was still waving from her front porch until the car turned the corner.

Maddy felt comfortable again when she was out of her mother's sight and turned to April. She looked wholesomely pretty, as usual. Maddy could never pull that look off.

"Hey," April said.

"Hey," Maddy replied. "Thanks Mrs. Burton—for the lift."

"No worries. It's easy for me. I take April anyway, so it's no trouble picking you up, too. How was your vacation?"

They hadn't seen each other for the entire Christmas vacation, but they talked on the phone a lot. April's family had taken her to some special doctor who did a bunch of tests to see about her sight briefly returning. It had faded again, but her mother grasped to the little bit of hope it had given her. If April could see, she could stop blaming herself for April's blindness. But, like all good things, it didn't last. April didn't seem to care much. She said it was neat to see, but Maddy got the feeling she didn't see things the way everyone else did, even when she had had her sight back for that day. Mystical sight wasn't natural—it was supernatural.

Of course, April hadn't told her mother about San Francisco. April had told her mother she had fallen and hit her head while playing at Maddy's. Then Presto. She could see. Her mother bought it. She was just so thrilled at the thought of April's sight returning, she didn't question it. Neither April's nor Maddy's mother ever found out they were out of town that day or that they had come face to face with a psychotic vampire. As far as the moms were concerned, they stayed overnight at the other's house.

"It was okay, I guess."

"Ready to go back to school?"

That was the question of the day.

"I guess," Maddy answered the question for what felt like the tenth time.

"I sure am," April added. "I can't wait to see Cullen again. I've missed you both so much!"

She was as cheerful as ever. Sometimes Maddy thought that not being able to see gave her a sort of freedom from cultural pressures. No crash diets or fad hairdos. No keeping up with cover models and movie stars. Lucky girl.

"Yeah, me too, I guess. I certainly had enough of family for a while."

April's mom turned into the parking lot just in time for Maddy to see Cullen disappear behind the glass-paned front doors of the Eel River Community School. She got out, smoothed down her mini kilt, and waited for April to take her arm. They walked up the stairs together and into the building, talking about their hopes and fears for the day away from parental ears.

The three didn't get a chance to talk until lunch.

"Hey," Maddy said to Cullen as she and April sat down. Maddy flung her backpack off onto the floor and opened it. Cullen watched as she took her cool lunch box out of it and set it on the table. He wished he had a coolio lunch box like that. He had a reused paper bag from Burger King. His lunch wasn't from Burger King, though. It was a bag taken from the pile in Frank's car.

"I can't believe Mr. Ferguson already gave us homework on the first day back!" Maddy said gruffly.

"Yep." April added. "Mrs. Palamore, too."

"And we have to read three chapters in History! Mr. Grimm's trippin'! What does it matter what happened a hundred years ago anyway. And the day's just half over!" Maddy concluded.

"I bet Ms. MacFey won't give us homework on the first day," Cullen said.

"Bet she will," Maddy replied.

Maddy opened her lunch box and took out a little juice box, a neat ziplock back of veggie chips, and a sandwich on some sort of hearty whole grain bread, also contained in a clean ziplock.

"So," April said as she opened her own lunch bag. It was pink, of course, and it looked like a traditional brown bag, only it was made of some kind of thermal plastic stuff that kept the food fresh.

"So?" Maddy replied. She popped the tiny straw into the juice box and sipped it. Her big green eyes fixed on April.

"How are you two?" April continued.

"Um. Fine." Maddy said with one eyebrow cocked.

Turning to Cullen, April asked, "has Rowan come back—or out again?"

"No," Cullen said shortly. He *knew* they were going to want to talk about this again. He didn't volunteer the information about talking with Rowan briefly this morning or being magically cured from his cold. They didn't even know he had been sick anyway. Better just not to say anything.

"Haven't we talked about this enough?" Maddy said. "First with Ms. MacFey before break and then us again and again. It's all we ever talk about!" She began tapping her white-tipped black fingernails on the lunch table in frustration.

Cullen beamed at her. Maybe she had had enough of this conversation, too. He was immediately grateful to her and noticed how lovely she looked today. She wore a black choker with a pentagram set in a bottlecap as a charm. Her black net shirt fell off one shoulder revealing a temporary tattoo of a spider.

Maddy turned to him with a scowl, and Cullen looked down quickly, blushing.

"Well, yes, but it was a big deal after all! I mean, our lives are different now," April said.

"How?" Maddy retorted. "How are they different? You can't see anymore and my life is *exactly* the same. Believe me. If I had any kind of powers, I would change a few things."

Cullen remembered what Rowan had said about responsibility on the way to school. He saw the anger in Maddy's eyes and understood that a little bit.

"Okay, but what about Rowan? He's still inside you, right?" April asked Cullen.

"Yeah. He's still there." Cullen just wanted to hide. He opened his lunch sack and peered inside, as if he wanted to crawl in next to his sandwich.

April refused to drop it. "Well why do you think he's staying hidden? I mean, she's still out there, right? Someone has to stop her before she hurts more people."

The anger crept back in. "We don't know where she is, do we? She's been doing this for centuries, what makes you think we can stop her?" Cullen said, pulling out his peanut butter and jelly on white. It was smashed down so thin, that it almost looked like dough instead of bread.

"We almost stopped her the last time," April reminded them.

"But we didn't," Maddy said. "She got away. There are lots of kinds of evil in this world, April, and it doesn't just come in the form of vampires." She lowered her voice to a whisper when she said the word vampires. She tugged at the skeleton arm coverings, pulling them up a little higher.

"Yes, but—"

"But nothing. It's over. If she comes back, we'll deal. If we have to. That's the best you can do in this life—deal with things as they come," Maddy said, then took a bite of her sandwich. Baked tofu on whole grain bread. "Ugh," she said. Grimacing, she dropped it.

Cullen looked at Maddy's sandwich and then back at his own.

"Trade ya," Maddy said to Cullen.

"Okay." Cullen was happy to eat something healthier than PB&J on white. He took a bite of the baked tofu. Yum! It had sprouts, too!

They all ate in silence for a few minutes. They used to have so much else to talk about, but now it was only about this. Why couldn't they talk more about school or Christmas or anything but this? Cullen was just about to bring up Christmas, although he of course didn't really get anything but a candy cane and some new underwear, but he loved to see April smile; she had such a pretty smile. Maybe she had a really great Christmas, but as he opened his mouth to speak, April spoke first:

"He's really been hiding this whole time?"

"Yep, and it's fine by me. He can stay hidden."

He felt Rowan retreat so deep into his mind, it was like he wasn't even there.

CHAPTER FIVE

Northern California, 1860 A. D. Wesh-et-wah braced himself against the trunk of a redwood, struggling with his guilt and despair. They had not set out to cause more death and destruction, but to try to prevent it. They had failed horribly. They may have safeguarded themselves, but only by destroying more innocent people. They had not gone out prepared for a fight. With the white man so close, they should always be prepared for a fight. How had they not yet learned that?

The visions of the carnage filled Wesh-et-wah's mind like a virus spreading into his soul. They had done this. They had taken an innocent tribe's protection and in doing so left them vulnerable. Sickened beyond endurance, he fell to his knees and vomited into the bracken. It was his body's futile attempt to purge his soul. He could still smell the rank, metallic blood stench. He could still hear the screams. He had been selfish, and now all those people were dead. Many other husbands would return to find their wives and daughters dead, their lives ruined. The fundamental rightness of their world, destroyed. Perhaps destroyed beyond repair.

He looked down at the strange knotty wood in disgust. He didn't even want it anymore. He had half a mind to toss it into the river where no one could find it. He was overcome by grief, but he wasn't a fool. If this could protect them—if this could protect his son—then not all would be lost. If nothing else, perhaps it would give them enough time to find an effective way to defeat these death-bringers. If they just had more time to prepare, but there was no preparing against such savagery.

Wesh-et-wah stood up and breathed in deeply, trying to clear the smell of blood and vomit from his lungs. He needed to be strong. There were still a few left who could be saved. He needed to do what he could for them. For his son.

He moved on.

Upon returning to camp, he mutely approached the shaman. She was carving the face of a man onto the lid of a box, an old man who's features were composed of leaves. Silently he handed her the talisman. She put down her carving, so similar to the one Wesh-et-wah had left behind in the Winnau village. Taking the strange, knotty piece of wood reverently, she closed her eyes, inhaling deeply.

"I can feel its power, Wesh-et-wah," she said.

Wesh-et-wah looked at her blankly. "They came. Right after we left with this, they came," he said sadly.

A look of horror spread across her face. "And the Winnau?"

"All the women and young girls are dead, killed within minutes." Tears ran down his rust-colored cheek. He knew how the returning Winnau men would feel upon seeing the nightmare that awaited them. He knew first hand, and this time he was partially responsible. Bracing himself for the next wave of grief, he turned away. "I must rest now. Do what you will with this talisman. I will have no more of it."

The shaman nodded in understanding, and Wesh-et-wah ducked into his dwelling to find his son sleeping. It was all for him, after all; but now there are more orphans because they stole the talisman. What kind of world was this where men killed others so brutally? Where men killed unarmed children and women? What reason could explain such savagery?

But there was no reason to any of it.

These white men were not reasonable; there could be no justifiable objective for such vicious behavior. They held their own brand of insanity, birthed from the hunger for more power and control. Logic and insanity do not mix.

He curled up next to his son and tried to sleep, but he could not silence the echo of their screams. He vainly covered his ears and tried to focus on the distant drumbeat. The shaman would go on a journey quest tonight for guidance, and the cadence of the drum would guide her to the netherworld to meet with her spirit guides.

Wesh-et-wah focused his attention on the drums, determined to go on a journey quest of his own. He shut his eyes tight and let his mind formulate the entrance to the underworld. For him, it was through one of the mighty redwoods. Several of the older and larger trees' trunks had split, so it was an opening, like a cave. In his mind's eye, he went into this wooden cave, and it led him into the netherworld. He saw himself slip down between the roots of the trees into the majesty of the underworld. All the animals below would come out from hiding to see who had come to visit. Crossing a narrow river took him to the place in the nether-forest where he met his spirit guide: Moose.

The moose ambled up slowly to where Wesh-et-wah stood and nuzzled his big nose against Wesh-et-wah's cheek. Wesh-et-wah honored the moose by petting the side of the moose's sizable nose. The stately moose bowed his head and allowed Wesh-et-wah to stroke his magnificent antlers.

Ask your question, the moose thought to Wesh-et-wah.

"Great Moose," Wesh-et-wah said to his spirit guide, "what are we to do? I tried to help our tribe by taking the talisman, and now so many others are dead."

The moose nodded slowly, and replied, *It was not yours to take, Wesh-et-wah. It was not the Winnau's to keep either.*

Wesh-et-wah knew the moose spoke the truth.

There is only one thing to do, for the greater good of all...

"We must bury it," said the white man. He was no longer tied, as he had earned their trust. He sat next to the shaman by the fire and spoke gently to her as she continued to carve the leafy-man's face into the new box.

The shaman looked at him as if he was something other than human, which she knew he was.

"This will protect us from your kind. We will not bury it but keep it among us. You heard what Wesh-et-wah said happened after he took it from the Winnau people. We will be safe with it here."

"They are not my kind," he said and turned away from her, as if he didn't hear anything else she had said.

Having this white man around constantly reminded her and her tribe of the white man's cruelty, but she could feel the goodness in this one. This one had a purpose, and he wanted peace as well. The firelight accented the lines on his face making him look very old and very sad. She knew him to be a gentle man. But they must be on their guard. He was still a white man after all. She remained wary. "They are the white man. You are a white man. They are your people," she reasoned.

"They are not my people. My skin may be white, but my people are ancient—as ancient as these trees that surround us."

"What stories you tell, Arthur," she said shaking her head. She laughed to herself and continued carving, but knew he did not lie. And that frightened her. She wondered how he could be as old as the trees, but she new he was not of this world. He was from the netherworld or some other such supernatural place.

She could feel it. She could see it in his eyes and hear it in his voice. Yes, this white man was very, very old.

The knotty wooden talisman sat in her lap, nearly camouflaged with the tanned skin of her dress. She caught Arthur eyeing it when she glanced back at him. The lines of tiny polished bones that adorned her bodice began to weigh down on her shoulders. Her strength of will faltered. Had she misjudged this white man?

An instant of fear shot through her heart.

If he was from the netherworld, he had more power than she. Why hadn't he used it to get away or to defend himself? Perhaps she should listen to this white man.

"I will listen, Arthur. Tell me more of your people."

Arthur hesitated and looked up into the night sky, as if he was trying to decide where to begin. After a long pause, during which the shaman put down her carving and waited patiently, Arthur began.

"My people are ancient. The story of my kind is no longer important, as we have faded even beyond memory. But you must know that we, too, were victims of cruel white men, other white men in another time. He who is in that wand, this talisman, was also a victim. He and his wife, long, long ago. Their lives were destroyed by these other white man, just as your lives have been destroyed by white men today. It is his life and his story which is important now. His story is important to us all."

Phiculoks-Kabuc saw the regret in his eyes and exhaled the breath she hadn't been aware she held. This man had seen much pain as well.

"Tell me the story of this man, Arthur"

"Let me show you."

He touched the Shaman's arm, and she felt a surge of power similar to what she tasted when she touched the talisman. Arthur did not need to speak this story, for he wove a tale she could see and feel. She actually saw the story unfold in images, first in her head and then as if they were all around her—consuming her.

She saw the wedding in the circle of tall stones.

She saw the Green Man and Green Woman with their fiery hair kiss and embrace.

She saw the white strangers come and kill.

She saw the bride escape into the netherworld and the man left behind, forced to hide in the knotty wood.

She saw the fat monk carry the wand away.

The images moved faster and faster. They made her dizzy as she watched the bride return and search and search and search. The ages passed, but she did not age. She saw the unseen cost propel her down towards darkness. She saw the Sons of Fey as dogs, then as men. Arthur was one of these men. She saw the moroi turn the bride into a soulless monster, the final fall. And she understood why the talisman had to be protected.

She understood why Arthur had sworn to shield it.

She understood the importance to all life.

Arthur released her arm, and she had to steady herself. Her carving fell from her lap and onto the forest floor. The talisman fell next to the carved box.

"This woman, she is close?"

"Perhaps. She must not find it, ever. If they are reunited, she will be too powerful, and we will all perish." Arthur held his hands up to the fire, as if chilled by what he had revealed. The memory of the pain, the sacrifice, and the endless searching made him feel the coldness of despair.

"Yes, but it will protect us. How can we deny ourselves that after all we have seen? After all the white man has done to my people?"

"If she is close, she will be able to feel it. If she finds you with it, you will have wished you died quickly at the hands of the white man. You have not seen brutality or cruelty until you meet her kind. We must hide it from her."

"But how, if she can feel it? Even if we hide it—"

"We must hide it from the eye of all, but also from her black heart. I believe with our combined powers we can create a barrier around it, a magical barrier that even she cannot penetrate. A strong barrier that she cannot even see."

"The white man will come."

"That is inevitable, no matter what you do. The time to change that is long past."

"I see the need," she told Arthur. "We must allow an evil to prevail to prevent a worse one, but my tribe will not understand. If we do this, we must do it alone, without their knowledge, save Wesh-et-wah. He has earned his place. Even though we will leave them with nothing, we will not take their hope."

"Let it be thusly," said Arthur.

"We will die," she said without emotion, resigned to their fate.

"Then I will die with you," Arthur said.

The following day, Phiculoks-Kabuc explained the situation to Wesh-et-wah, and he did not like it after the slaughter he had seen the previous night but agreed, as it was the same thing his spirit guide had advised him.

He was just so tired.

He had endured more in the past weeks than most do in a lifetime. Perhaps it was best that he die soon, for this was no longer a world he recognized. It was not a world he wished for his son either.

The three hiked through the forest together—Wesh-et-wah, Phiculoks-Kabuc, and Arthur, searching for the perfect place. The ferns that spread over the floor of the redwood forest glowed ethereally bright in the misty dank moonlight filtering through the trees. They walked for what seemed like hours, until the moon was high in the sky. Finally, they came upon an ancient grove. The trunk of the largest tree among them was split into an opening, like a small cave. Wesh-et-wah recognized it from his journey the previous night. It was the exact tree that he saw in his mind's eye. The one that led him into the netherworld.

"This is the place," the shaman said, validating Wesh-et-wah's thoughts. "It will have the added protection of this tree, for we will bury it within its heart."

Arthur said, "It is a good place, reverent. It's fitting as the final resting place for this unfortunate soul."

Phiculoks-Kabuc took the talisman from her waistband. She had a strange expression on her face, something between great respect and great fear. Pressing the talisman between her palms, she touched the tip of it to her forehead and then her lips. Then, bobbing in tiny bows over it, she muttered her sacred words.

Wesh-et-wah heard drums and a pipe in the distance. Perhaps they played only in his mind. He knew they would die soon, but all must die eventually. It is the natural way. He found that he was no longer afraid of death, but rather prepared for it. He closed his eyes and offered his soul up to the Great Spirit in the silent sanctuary of his mind. When he opened his eyes again, he saw the shaman crawling inside the tree cave. There, with the help of a flat stone, she dug a hole and placed the talisman within the earth. With a few other soft-spoken words, which Wesh-et-wah could not hear but knew to be magcial, she laid her hands on top of the sacred spot and bowed low to the ground. Wesh-et-wah bowed his head in respect.

"It is done," she said, kneeling in the mouth of the tree-cave. She brushed the dirt from her hands and tried to stand. But she faltered a little, as if her bones were stiff from kneeling in such a small place. Wesh-et-wah thought it might be because she, too, knew they would soon die.

"It is not enough," Arthur said. His face showed no emotion. Not sadness or fear. His expression was just empty.

"I have said the words of concealment over it, and now we must also make this area invisible to her and to any with a black heart or malicious intentions."

"Wait. I'll put our protection on the wand as well, and then we will hide this entire grove together with both our magics," Arthur said. He moved over to the mouth of the cave and took out a knife. He carved something into the trunk, but Wesh-et-wah could not read what it said. They were strange crosshatching-like marks, perhaps a kind of ancient language.

"Wesh-et-wah," the shaman said, "stand outside the grove."

Wesh-et-wah obeyed. He could already feel the magic within this sacred place. The trill of the pipe filled his mind again, but it did not come from outside of him. The beat of the drum strengthened his resolve, as this ritual sealed their fate.

The shaman and white man circled around the huge tree in ever widening rings, murmuring their words of magic in their separate languages. The sound of the drums and pipe filled the grove, playing from nowhere. Now, joining those sounds he held so dear was another sound. It merged in perfectly, although the sound was quite foreign to Wesh-et-wah. It was a kind of pipe, but edgier with a constant sustained note behind the melody. Sad and beautiful at the same time, Wesh-et-wah felt the tears on his cheek again. This must be the sound of magic from Arthur's people, and magical it was. The most magical sound Wesh-et-wah had ever heard.

When Arthur and the shaman got to the edge of the grove, the music stopped.

"It is done," the shaman said again, "We must go back and face our fate alone."

Leading Wesh-et-wah with a gentle touch on his arm, the shaman guided him away from the place.

Arthur followed in silence.

Wesh-et-wah looked back once more but could no longer see the grove. They had not traveled so far, but he could not see it. He recognized the surrounding trees and foliage, but it was as if the grove had slipped into nothingness.

The spell had worked.

They returned to their camp to find the white man already there.

CHAPTER SIX

Mr. Ferguson peered out of his classroom window to watch Ms. MacFey walk into the teachers' lounge—right on schedule. Everyday he watched her go from her classroom to the teachers' lounge for more coffee. She was wearing his favorite blue jean skirt and a red blouse, as if the Christmas spirit still lived in her heart even after the new year. Her chestnut hair fell softly over her shoulders. She was pure grace. When she was out of sight, he turned from the door, removed his pocket protector, laid it on his desk, took a deep breath, straightened his tie, and smoothed back his hair. He was going to do it this time. He was finally going to ask her out.

As he entered the teachers' lounge, Ms. MacFey was pouring herself a cup of coffee. She looked so lovely today, just as she always did. The morning sun spilled through the window and illuminated her hair. He imagined that it smelled like lavender.

"Good morning, Ms. MacFey," he said.

Max looked over her shoulder and smiled. "Ralph, I've told you a hundred times to call me Max. You aren't one of my students."

"Of course, Max," he said, blushing slightly. "How were your holidays?" He moved beside her in front of the coffee station. His collar already felt a little hot. He picked up the coffee cup covered in math equations, with $C = 2\pi r$ most prominently displayed, and poured himself a cup. The school didn't have throw-away coffee cups. Each teacher had to bring their own personal cup. Max's was blue and the words "Manifest Your Own Destiny" were written in a very flowy white font. They both reached for the sugar at the same time, causing Ralph to pull his hand back quickly, embarrassed. He pushed his glasses up and took a step back.

"No, you go ahead. I need to cut down on it anyway. Too much chocolate over the holidays," she said as she picked up the nonfat creamer and shook the clumpy dry powder into the blackness of her coffee.

"You like chocolate?" Ralph said reaching for the sugar again with his face still flushed red. He tipped the round cardboard container and let sugar spill into his coffee for a moment before putting it back down.

"Dark especially. Girl's best friend," Max said smiling while stirring her coffee. She was several inches shorter than he was, and he loved the way she looked up at him. It made her eyes the first thing he noticed, and she did have such lovely eyes. More amber than brown. Every glorious color of autumn danced in the delight her eyes.

"I'll have to remember that," Ralph replied pushing up his glasses again nervously and smiling.

"Why?"

Flustered, he splashed coffee on his tie.

"Of course," he said under his breath. He grabbed a brown paper napkin from off the table. There were no white ones, as the school took their environmental pledge very seriously. He blotted his tie with the 60% post-consumer recycled brown napkin, which turned slightly darker brown with the coffee he mopped up.

"And it's not even Monday," Max said playfully, touching his arm and laughing. "I usually do things like that on Mondays. I swear—the number of times I've had to change my blouse."

Ralph laughed along with her, though now he had to deal with the image of Max removing her blouse in the teachers' lounge, which only increased his nervousness. Despite his mini klutz-o-rama, she was so easy to talk to. She would probably say yes, wouldn't she? Even if it was just out of pity. Their laughter died and she stood there with her hands wrapped around her coffee mug for warmth. The sound of her carefree laugh had boosted his confidence, so he took a step forward.

"Um…" Ralph said, throwing away the coffee-stained napkin he used to blot his tie, careful to put it in the trash can and not the recycling bin right next to it. "I—I was wondering."

Max, sipping her coffee, looked at him over her coffee cup. Her amber eyes were so big and sweet. He could look into them all day.

The bell rang, and he breathed easier. What a cliché. He took a step back and pushed up his glasses again. Bowing his head and staring into the onyx abyss in his coffee mug he said, "Nothing."

"Ok—well, I'm off to class. See you later?" Max said.

"You got it," he replied with an awkward wave. Really? With the goofy wave, too? "Smooth move…" he mumbled to himself as she left. Shaking his head at his own oafishness, he went off to class.

He liked his job overall, even though he taught mostly algebra and geometry. Physics was his passion, and the Eel River Community School allowed him one physics class a year. It was by far his favorite to teach, although it was little more than talking at a roomful of raging hormones who had no interest in the fascinating secrets of the cosmos. One more algebra class to get through before lunch, and then he would see Max again.

As he entered his classroom, a paper airplane hit him on the nose.

CHAPTER SEVEN

The dissonant sounds of Eel River students sharing stories of their holidays or engaging in random juvenile hazings filled the cafeteria. Max passed by Cullen, Maddy, and April just as Maddy and Cullen exchanged sandwiches. They didn't see her, so she didn't wave. They were a daily reminder of the traumatic events of last fall, but they were good kids. As if she could forget being attacked by a vampire anyway. She sat down at the teacher's table across from Ralph who squeezed his juice box a little too hard, making it squirt on his coffee-stained tie. At least it was a dark color. She opened the little plastic container full of organic strawberry yogurt and sprinkled some granola on the top.

"Um. Max?" Ralph said.

Max looked up from stirring her yogurt at Ralph who was still wiping juice from his tie, but something caught her eye over his shoulder at the far end of the cafeteria.

A jolly man stood there looking around as if taking in the entire place before deciding what to do next. He rapped his thick fingers on his large belly. He was leaning back slightly and seemed to taper off at each end. He wore a new three-piece pin-striped suit and a smart fedora hat. It took her a minute to recognize him.

"I—I was wondering, maybe if you wanted to—" Ralph said.

"Sorry Ralph, I'll be right back," she said, not noticing the hurt look on Ralph's face; she got up immediately to greet this bizarre, well-dressed man.

She found herself trying very hard not to run over to him. He saw her coming and smiled a wide smile. He held out his arms to welcome her. Throwing her arms around his neck, she said, "Moody! It is so wonderful to see you! Where have you been? Ohmygosh you look great!" she said. And he did. First of all, he was clean. Really clean. New suit. New hat. That horrid dead-fish smell that had wafted off of him all the way back from San Francisco, her car still didn't smell quite right, was completely gone. He smelled like...daisies!! He was also devoid of his feline entourage. *Perhaps it was the fish smell that had kept them around,* she thought, but then she saw the head of an orange and white kitten peeking out from his coat pocket.

"Here and there, dear girl. Here and there." He cupped her face in his hands and looked intently at her. Momentarily touching his bulbous nose against hers, he said, "It's good to see you again."

"I missed you," she said, and she truly meant it. That surprised her.

"Yes. I did take off rather suddenly, but having a clear mind again allowed me to remember something very important. I needed to take care of it," he explained, dropping his hands from her face and smoothing down his lapels.

"Well what was so important you couldn't say goodbye?" she asked, crossing her arms rather crossly. It had been quite rude of him, especially after all they had been through together.

Before Moody could answer, Cullen, Maddy, and April plowed into him and all gave him a big hug at once, making a ring around his considerable belly with their arms interlocked.

There was plenty of middle for all of them.

"Holy Mackerelandy!" he exclaimed.

"Where did you go?" Cullen said.

"Yeah, you just disappeared," Maddy added.

The kids stepped back and Moody bent over to look into Cullen's eyes.

"Where are you Green Man? I don't see you."

"What!" Ms. MacFey said, spinning Cullen to face her. Hands on his shoulders, she bent over to look into his eyes herself, as if she could see Rowan even if he was there.

"Oh, he's still there all right," Cullen said sullenly, "He's just in deep hiding."

Max let go of Cullen and standing up, noticed that other students were beginning to talk and point, so Max said, "Perhaps here is not the place for this discussion. Can you all meet at my place after school?"

"Fa-bu-lous idea, my dear. Fa-bu-lous!" he said and pulled out a new golden pocket watch. Popping it open he said, "Say, four o'clock?"

"Better make it 4:30," Max said, "Kids?"

"Yep," said Maddy.

"Sure," said April.

"Um," said Cullen.

"What's the problem? You're not still grounded are you?" Maddy asked with her hands on her hips in a disturbingly parental way.

"Yeah. Okay, I'll be there."

"You better be, young man! You better be! Much, much to discuss!" Moody said, replacing his pocket watch and then rapping his fingers on his massive belly. "Toodle-loo!"

With that, he spun around on his heels and strode out of the cafeteria.

What a strange man, Max thought.

The kids were already headed back to their table, so she headed back to hers and once again sat across from Ralph, who looked rather glum.

"Who was that?" he asked, pushing his glasses up nervously and sounding a little jealous.

"My uncle," Max said, smiling to herself. It was so cool to have such a bizarre uncle, especially when she hadn't know he existed until just two months ago. He looked so great today, a far cry from the homeless man they found on the streets of San Francisco last November.

"You wanted to ask me something? I'm so sorry I interrupted you. I just hadn't seen him in a while, and it was kinda a surprise to see him here. Sorry if I was rude, but you can ask me now." Max picked up the rest of her yogurt to finish her lunch, and gave Ralph her undivided attention.

"It can wait," Ralph said, looking down at his empty juice box.

After school, Max took the freshly baked cookies out of the oven and set them on the stovetop to cool. She stirred the three cups of hot cocoa and added tiny marshmallows to each before carrying them out to the table on a tray. Just as she set them down, there was a knock on the door.

"Come in," she said and then cringed. She should know better than to invite anyone in without some definite proof of who they were. With that thought, her hand went unconsciously to the scar on her neck. But all was good; the three kids came in, said their hellos, and started piling their coats on the couch. Max had started a fire to make it all nice and homey for her coming visitors. It was so nice to have company. And it was so rare that she went all out even for casual visitors.

"Where's Moody," Cullen asked.

"He's not here yet, but I've got some hot chocolate for you guys. That should warm you right up."

Maddy led April over to the table and helped her find her chair before taking her own. As Cullen passed, Max reached out and tussled his hair.

"How is my little knight? Have a good holiday?"

"Um, it was okay. Quiet." He seemed different somehow. Not adorably awkward as usual, but rather cold and distant. She feared that these strange events were changing him.

Another knock shifted her attention away from her young guests. This time she walked over to the door and looked through the peep hole. There she saw the fish-eyed shape of Moody and smiled at how the peep hole glass exaggerated his already unique form. She opened the door and he strode by her confidently, thumbs tucked into the sides of his vest.

"Thank you, thank you, Miss," he said as he took off his hat and placed it on top of a lamp shade. He turned back and gathered up Max into a huge bear hug. She couldn't help but laugh, her body bent around his big middle.

"It's good to be home," Moody sighed.

"It's good to have you home," Max squeaked from inside the embrace.

Moody released her and said, "Something smells great!"

"Hungry?"

"I could eat. I can always eat!"

Shadow, Max's cat, emerged sleepily from behind the sofa, stretched grandly, reaching one arm out further than it should go and then the other. She yawned widely, curling her tongue, then jumped up into Moody's arms. He placed her on his shoulder, where she snuggled against his neck and resumed her afternoon nap.

"Come in and have a seat. What about a drink?"

"A cup of tea would be lovely, my dear."

"Coming right up." Max left them all at the table and went into the kitchen to make his tea and grab some other goodies. She could hear them talking in the next room. Her house wasn't that big after all. They said their hellos and how-are-yous, but it didn't take Moody long to bring up Rowan. She heard Cullen almost shout, "I don't want to talk about it!"

"What's going on?" she said as she set Moody's tea before him and a plate full of cookies in the center of them all.

"Thank you, dear."

"What's going on," she repeated.

"Cullen is sick of talking about Rowan," April said with her arms crossed over her chest. "He was the same way at lunch today."

"I don't blame him," Maddy chimed in, grabbing a cookie. "I mean—it's over with. Why do we have to go over and over and over it, through it again and again and again? Let's just move on."

"Yeah. Let it go already." Cullen said.

Max had never seen Cullen so stern, and she wondered if his sweetness would ever return. Had he already suffered too much?

Moody just sat in silence, listening patiently. Shadow snoozed soundly, purring against his neck. Moody helped himself to a cookie and dipped it in his tea until it was thoroughly soaked and pieces began to fall off, making little cookie islands.

"I'm sorry," Cullen said at last. "It's just been weird, you know? I just want it to be over. I mean, you would think having a powerful wizard with you all the time would be great an' all. You'd think I could give all the bullies a what for, but it really is only constant danger and fear. Not to mention the complete absence of privacy."

This declaration made Max very sad. She had never thought about it that way. Although she would like to have Rowan around all the time herself, there were still private moments that everyone should have. But poor Cullen not only lost his real family and had to live with a horrible foster family, but he also had to deal with this supernatural entity in his brain. Poor kid.

"That's what I want to talk about," Moody said. "We all need to go back to where you found the wand, Cullen. I need to feel if there is any magical signature left that might help me with some questions. There might be a way to let Rowan finally rest in the Otherworld, thus separating the two of you."

"What?" Max said. She didn't want to think about Rowan leaving this world for good. "Don't we need him to defeat Fiana?"

"Perhaps, but she may be too powerful for that. Her power grew tenfold after Cullen released Rowan from his wand. If she gets her way and turns Rowan, it will destroy Cullen, but that will be the least of our worries."

Cullen's face turned white.

"Don't worry, lad, we'll work it out," Moody said, patting Cullen's hand reassuringly. "We'll keep you safe. But the best way to do that is to get Rowan out of you and where he belongs: in the Otherworld with the rest of his people. Then we'll deal with Fiana. She'll still be powerful, but having him in this dimension increases her power, and if she does turn him and they truly unite, they will be more powerful together than this world has ever known. They will not only destroy Cullen. They will destroy us all."

Everyone was silent for a very long time.

"But how can you know this?" April said.

"Holy Mackerelandy! Can't you see it for yourself?

"I can't. That power faded over a couple of days," she replied matter-of-factly. She didn't seem to care one way or the other.

"Wait," Max said trying to comprehend, "You're saying Rowan must die?"

"No! I mean, I don't want him in my head more than you know, but I don't want him to die either!" Cullen said.

Moody looked at him solemnly, his face very gentle. "What kind of life do you suppose this is for him, Cullen? Living inside a young boy such as yourself? He deserves some peace, some rest."

"How would that work?" Maddy asked. "I mean, would we have to kill him?"

"No, no, my dear. We must just lead Cullen into the Otherworld."

"Okay—this is officially crazy. You're not taking a child into the land of the dead," Max said strictly. What was he thinking? No way would she let him put Cullen in danger like that, and this had nothing to do with how much she wanted to see Rowan again. It would be great if he could somehow separate them, then Rowan could live here with them all and start a new life. She even had an extra room. (Surely a fourteen-hundred-year separation counted as a divorce.)

"The Otherworld is not merely the realm of the dead, it is also the home of the Sidhe and the gods. Rowan is out of his time here. He is out of place. He needs to be with his people," Moody said.

"But—" Max began, but before she could finish her thought, Cullen interrupted.

"We have a while to think about it before we decide. The veil doesn't open until Halloween. That's what Rowan told me," Cullen said.

"But he and Fiana opened it the night she escaped, and that wasn't Halloween," April said.

"That's true, but they are very powerful together. I do not have the kind of power Fiana has," Moody explained, "but that doesn't mean I am without power. I believe that we may be able to open it on another feast day. The old ways had four major feast days throughout the year. Four major and four minor ones. The others aren't as powerful as Samhain, but it may be enough for Rowan and I to combine our powers and open the veil. It's worth a shot."

"When is the next one?" Max said.

"Imbolc," Maddy answered, "February first is the next."

They all looked at her impressed.

She beamed.

"Very good, my dear," Moody replied. "She is correct. Imbolc is the next, then Beltane after that, Lughnasadh, and back to Samhain."

"Okay, February first. So that gives us about three weeks to decide," Max said, "but shouldn't Rowan get a say in this? Is he listening, Cullen? What does he say?"

"He's not listening. He's deep inside brooding somewhere," he replied, rolling his eyes. "But I'll see about trying to get through to him over the next few weeks. Maybe I can talk with him in a dream like I used to."

"Fa-bu-lous!" Moody exclaimed, clasping his hands together in agreement. "But we can't just wait! Oh no! We all have work to do to prepare! Maddy, you must find out all you can about Imbolc and its rituals. It has been a long time for me, so I need someone else to know. Can you do that?"

"Absolutely!" Maddy said. She was smiling even bigger than before, her green eyes bright and full of excitement.

"April, I need you to focus on your new power."

April began to protest, but Moody stopped her. "I know you say it has left you, but it hasn't. It remains, and you must work on strengthening it."

"Okay. I'll try."

"I'll help," Maddy said. "I know some spells and meditations and stuff. It'll help me focus on mine, too."

"These might also help," Moody said, reaching into his pocket. He pulled out a small velvet drawstring bag and placed it in April's hand.

"What's this," April said.

Maddy opened the bag for her and turned it upside down, spilling the contents onto the table. They looked like thick twigs, all of the same basic size and shape. Some of the bark was carved off in the middle and a strange symbol was burned into the wood. Maddy spread them out over the table. Each twig bore a different symbol.

"Runes?" Maddy said.

"That's right, my dear. Runes," Moody replied.

"What are runes," April asked. Her fingers traced the shape of the twig and the strange symbol burned into its heart.

"It's a system of divination. I believe you have the gift of second sight. You are a seer, my dear, and these are the tools of a seer."

"Wow! Thanks!" April said.

"We'll get a book on runes and learn them together! I think my mom might have one," Maddy said.

"Fa-bu-lous," Moody said before turning to Cullen, letting April continue to explore her runes. "Cullen, of course you must speak with Rowan about the plan; but first we must return to where he was found. I will see what I can find from there, and then we'll know more about how to proceed."

"Why can't you go yourself. You found it well enough before."

"Cullen!" Max said, surprised. He was not acting like himself at all.

"It's fine, my dear," Moody said to her. Then to Cullen he explained, "I was able to find it on that night because it was full of Fiana and Rowan's magic. It was visible to any who could feel such things. The magic of that night broadcast out in powerful waves. Any third rate witch in Wichita could've felt it. Now, all that magic is not there. All that remains is the lingering magic of its former concealment spell. I felt something that night, underlying Rowan and Fiana's magic, but I couldn't focus on it, as you remember. That was quite a night! I believe I can feel it if I get closer, but that is a big forest. Please take us all there, Cullen."

"Fine," Cullen said, crossing his arms.

Moody turned to Max.

She didn't know if she wanted to help, not with anything that would take Rowan away from her. She knew she was being selfish, but she didn't care. She was tired of being lonely, and she wanted to be with him. *Snap out of it*, she thought to herself, *of all the kids here you are acting like the biggest child.*

"Maxine," Moody said, "You and I will speak in private about this at another time. For now, finish up your warm drinks for we're about to go on a very cold journey."

CHAPTER EIGHT

"Hey! Careful with that," Fred said to Rex, who had found his mom's 9mm. "She keeps it loaded."

Rex carefully slid it back under the pile of blankets in her closet where he had found it. Fred had become a good deal more timid since his adventures as a rodent some months before. He gathered Rex was too. They didn't talk about that weird day in the boys' restroom last fall. They just pretended that a big wizard didn't turn Fred and Todd into mice and temporarily take Rex and Scott's mouths away. Best just to forget about it.

It wasn't what they were looking for anyway. Fred claimed his mother kept a bottle of brandy hidden in her bedroom. This is what they wanted. Everyone knew that teenagers drank, at least the cool ones did. And that included Rex and his gang, so they needed some alcohol. Todd and Scott were waiting for them in the park.

"Hey, is your dad taking you fishing this weekend?" Fred asked, as they continued their search. They went through everything but were very careful to put it all back as they found it.

"Yeah. Wanna come?"

"Heck yeah! Where you goin'?"

"Someplace on the reservation. We can spearfish there because it's like their culture or something. We're gonna use pitchforks," Rex snickered.

"Cool. Count me in. As long as your dad don't mind."

"Don't worry 'bout him. He likes you." Rex smirked at Fred. "No accountin' for taste."

Fred hit Rex on the arm. Rex hit Fred back a little harder. But even the sting on his arm couldn't take away the warm feeling in his chest. It wasn't easy for a boy to grow up without a father, especially in a back-woods, testosterone-riddled community like his. He looked up to Frank as a kind of surrogate. His mother never brought men home, which was really okay with him. He didn't need another parent. One was more than enough. Sometimes she would go out. Fred thought she might be meeting a man, but his mom never talked about it. Maybe she was meeting women! Fred shuddered at the thought.

Rex threw his arms up in exasperation and said, "It ain't here."

"Yeah," said Fred. "But it's got to be in her room somewhere. Maybe it's just not in the closet. I know she keeps it here."

"You try under her bed," Rex said, "I'll look through her drawers."

The gleam in Rex's eye and the smile he was trying to hide disgusted Fred. He knew what Rex was thinking, and it was gross. "Don't play with her panties."

"You're a sick bastard," Rex opened the top drawer, picked up a pair of pink panties and twirled them in the air.

Fred rolled his eyes. He lifted the bed skirt to peer beneath his mom's bed.

"My, my, my, Mrs. Taylor," Fred heard Rex say and just tried to ignore him.

There were several boxes under the bed. He pulled one out and continued to ignore Rex, who now wore some black lace panties on his face. There were some official-looking documents and lots of old pictures. The brandy was there too, but Fred was much more interested in the pictures. He tossed the brandy onto the bed and looked more closely at the photographs. His mom looked like a teenager, maybe just a few years older than he was now, and she was really pretty.

Rex jumped on the bed and said "Hey! You could've told me you found it!"

Frank looked up to see that Rex was panty-free now and holding the brandy.

"Look at these," Fred said, offering some pictures to Rex. "Don't that look like your dad?" Although Mr. Samuels was really fat now, in these pictures he was lean and muscular, clearly an athlete.

"Yep. That's him. Must've been taken back in Texas right after high school. He looks the same in pictures with me as a baby. Who's this woman?"

Fred didn't answer. He was too busy looking at his birth certificate. It was the first time he's ever seen it. There it was in black and white.

"Is that your mom?" Rex said. "Why's he with your mom?"

CHAPTER NINE

It was cold. Cullen shivered a little inside his over-sized, hand-me-down coat. The four others followed closely behind as he led them through the redwoods towards his secret grove. He didn't like having to reveal the only place that was truly his to them all, but he didn't have much choice. It would probably be worth it if it helped him get rid of Rowan.

The girls were chatting between themselves. Max and Moody were also talking about where he had gone and how he suddenly had so much money, something about World War I and bonds or something. Cullen wasn't really listening, but he was growing more annoyed by the minute.

They had no sense of reverence for the forest. No respect for its quiet nature. He looked over his shoulder and scowled as they prattled along behind him.

Just get this over with, he thought to himself. *Get rid of the wizard and the vampire will go away. Then I'll start reading mystery novels or maybe romance, but no more fantasy.*

Cullen was used to tolerating things he didn't like, but lately his temper was growing ever shorter. Perhaps if Rowan stayed away, he would have more control over his anger again. Although, Rowan had stayed hidden for six weeks before his appearance this morning. His absence had not noticeably improved Cullen's demeanor, quite the opposite really.

"Here it is," Cullen said, interrupting the chatter.

"Where did this tree come from? It wasn't here a minute ago! I swear!" Maddy said. "I would've noticed a tree this big."

"It's the concealment spell," Moody offered.

As Moody approached the tree to do his work, Maddy and April sat on a nearby fallen tree and continued to talk, as if they never had stopped. Maddy was talking in hushed, but excited tones about how she was sure her mother had a book of runes, and they could learn how to cast them together.

Max stayed back with Cullen a short way from the tree while Moody went up to it and ran his hands over the strange crosshatch-like lettering. Cullen couldn't help but laugh a little, watching oversized Moody try to get onto the ground and crawl into the tree-cave opening. Magic was definitely needed for that feat.

"It's nice to see you smile again, Cullen," Ms. MacFey said.

Cullen looked up at her, and his smile was already fading.

"This has been hard on you, hasn't it," Ms. MacFey said.

Well, duh, Cullen thought, but he didn't say anything. Talking serious with grown-ups always made him feel a little uncomfortable. It was not something he was used to, since any conversation with Trudy or Frank was pretty much them yelling and him just keeping quiet. He felt tears well up in his eyes, and he hated his body for reacting like that. He looked down quickly, trying to think of anything else. It seemed Moody's massive middle was stuck in the opening. That made him smile again.

"I don't blame you for not wanting to talk about it," Ms. MacFey continued, "but sometimes it helps to talk about things with the people who care about you."

Cullen just kept looking at Moody struggling to get back out of the tree. Had he really expected to fit? Now Maddy was laughing, too, and whispering to April, probably describing what she saw. April giggled.

"We all care about you, Cullen. We want to help. You know you can talk to me any time you like," Ms. MacFey said.

He really hoped she was finished.

Moody finally freed himself from the opening and landed hard on his backside, roaring with laughter himself.

"Come here kids. Come here!" he shouted over at them.

Cullen was happy to be rescued from the conversation. His feelings were his own. He didn't want to share them. Not with her. Not with anyone. As he walked towards Moody, who was dusting himself off, Maddy and April bounded past him, while Max followed pensively behind.

"Come closer! Come closer! Look here," he pointed to the strange cross-hatch writing over the tree's opening. "That is Ogham script. It is the ancient writing of the Druids."

"Rowan is a Druid!" Cullen said. "He told me. I Googled it. They lived a long time ago and worshipped trees and nature and stuff."

"Yes, like Rowan. Whoever hid the wand here knew what they were doing. I haven't seen that writing in a long time, and, although it's hard to tell since it's carved in a tree, I think it's my brother Arthur's hand. I feel his presence here, dimly, but it's here. Oh Arthur!" Moody exclaimed, with melancholy admiration. "Oh Arthur, it was you! You did what you set out to do!" he continued, shouting up to the heavens with dramatically outstretched arms, "you protected the wand for all these years. Oh brother, how I miss you!"

Cullen saw Moody wipe a tear from his eye, but without any embarrassment at the show of emotion. Despite his sometimes clownish behavior, Moody was a man—or fey, or elf, or whatever he really was—of noble stature.

"My brother was here. I can still feel his magic, but it is not just his magic! It is mixed with another powerful spell that kept it hidden for so long. In fact, I do not think I could've found it without you, Cullen! How did you ever find this place?"

Cullen felt put on the spot. "Um," he said, "I dunno. I just did one day."

"You were destined to find it, my boy. It's the only explanation, what with this concealment spell. This is your destiny, Cullen. You have magic in you, boy."

Cullen thought that was pretty cool overall. It must be why no one ever found him there and why he felt so safe there. It was magically protected!

"And see here," Moody continued, pointing inside the tree-cave, "this is where it was buried. Yes, here is where secret things are buried for safe-keeping." While Maddy and Ms. MacFey were looking into the tree cave, Moody winked at Cullen. Moody had found his special edition of *The Hobbit*! The book Ms. MacFey had given him for his birthday last year. The book he had to bury to keep Frank from burning with the others. He found it and he was going to keep his secret!

Cullen smiled.

It felt good to have a grown-up on his side. Well, two grown-ups counting Ms. MacFey. Maybe things were not all that bad.

"There is enough magic remaining here," Moody continued. "Yes! Yes! Enough magic here, with mine and Rowan's combined, to open the veil on Imbolc. I do think so. Okay!" he said, clapping his hands together. "Let us all get back to our homes and get to work. We have much to prepare for over the next few weeks!"

CHAPTER TEN

New York City, 1918 A. D. The streets were quiet, which was strange for a city this size. It had been like this for weeks. Quiet. Empty. Almost desolate. Once the workday ended, the city that never sleeps, slept. During the day, only those who had to be out were out—those that were not sick or didn't have sick loved ones. Those people were few and far between. The flu had hit hard this year. After only a month, more than thirty-thousand were dead from it.

The Germans were killing fewer in the trenches of Flanders.

Only one woman and one man were out on Broadway tonight. The woman, dressed in the latest fashion, twirled and danced down the middle of the street while the man, who was rather large around the middle and seemed to taper off at each end, slunk down the sidewalk near the buildings, keeping to the shadows while he followed her.

"What a night, Moody. What a beautiful night." Fiana's cheeks and lips looked more than just rosy—they were positively flush in full-bodied scarlet, even though she had not yet fed tonight. She had drunk her fill over the past few weeks, though, and would do so tonight as well. All this death provided a feast for her.

"Yes, my lady. The night is very beautiful. Quiet."

"Come here, Moody, I want to dance. No dance halls are open anymore, and I want to dance." She did love to dance. "All dressed up with no place to go." She pushed her bottom lip out in a phony pout.

Moody emerged from the shadows. He was also dressed to the nines in a three-piece black suit and a smart fedora. The pocket-watch chain tucked into his vest pocket bounced against his belly as he approached her. He loved when she was in a good mood and was nice to him. Two things that had been very rare as of late. In fact, it had been rare for as long as he could remember, but the past few weeks certainly had put a bounce back into her step. He just didn't like the reason why she was so happy.

Taking her in his arms, he spun her around in the middle of the road, nimbly avoiding the streetcar rails. He moved with the agility and grace of a man half his girth.

She laughed wildly, throwing her head back. Her fiery red hair was pulled up into a lovely twist, the single strands of white and black that framed her face when she wore her hair down now streaked up either side of her head. Short hair was in fashion, but she didn't care to cut her locks. Fashions were so fleeting. A small hat sat tilted on her head, held in place with a solid gold hat pin. Although she danced and spun on this cold night, not one hair fell out of place. She was exquisite.

"Where to tonight, my little Marlin?"

His heart filled with love for her. She was truly in a great mood if she was calling him Marlin! "Anywhere my lady desires. This city is yours," he responded as he twirled her in a spin, ending in a dramatic dip.

She laughed. The sound of her laughter filled his heart with joy and echoed off the vacant buildings. He led her into a promenade down Broadway, twirling and spinning in mirth.

"It's like a smorgasbord, Marlin! I can't drink fast enough! There is so much to choose from! This is the life! It's a great time to be ali—well, to be me!

Marlin stopped dancing with her suddenly, forcing Fiana to catch her balance, but she didn't miss a beat. She continued to dance as if led by an invisible stranger.

"I think I have the taste for something younger tonight. Have you heard the number of children orphaned because of this flu? I haven't seen anything like it since the Black Death, and I was in no position to enjoy it then—still obsessed with my pointless *quest*." She stopped dancing and walked back to Marlin. "But I am enjoying this to the fullest! Oh Marlin," she said clapping her hands together like a small child, "let's go to an orphanage tonight. I want to hear the little screams and drink something fresh."

"What?!"

He took her roughly by the arm and pulled her to the side of the street like he was afraid of being seen, even though there was no one around to see. He stopped in front of a window displaying some war posters. They were everywhere ever since the United States had entered the war the previous year. In this window, there were three: One, colored red, white, and blue, had the arms of Uncle Sam lighting a candle beneath the dome of the Capital, and the caption read: *Make this The Glorious 4th - Furnish the Fuse. BUY YOUR BONDS HERE*; the second bore a basket of fruits in front of a silhouette of men on horseback holding an American flag, caption: *Food is Ammunition—Don't*

Waste It; and the third poster featured a gaunt woman dressed all in black holding a baby close to her breast. Her arm was around another young, thin girl with her hand out. Behind this sad family were many, many people with their arms raised in the air against a backdrop of dilapidated buildings. The caption read: *Don't Waste Food While Others Starve!*

"Unhand me! How dare you manhandle me!" Fiana wasn't laughing now, squirming to break free of Marlin's grip. All the joy had drained from her eyes, and she clenched her teeth, glaring at Moody.

Surprisingly, he didn't let her go, but rather began to chide her.

"I won't stand for this anymore. You have gone too far. The city is in ruins. Look around you! People are dying by the thousands every day."

She stopped struggling. He continued:

"You can smell the death in the air and feel the collective suffering. It's bad enough that you feed on the sick and dying."

"Well," she said smiling and pointed to a window poster, "mustn't waste food now. We should do our part."

"Why must you add to it? You have fallen too far, my lady. Too far. I love you, of course, and I remain faithful to you, dear lady; but please, please stop being so cruel. There is plenty for you to eat without causing more suffering, especially in times like these." He shook her in his desperation and frustration, pleading with her.

"This isn't like you, Marlin. You've been moody for a long time, but you've never been foolish enough to question me like this." Fiana ripped her arm from his grasp. She was, after all, much stronger than Marlin. "Frankly," she continued, "I've long since grown weary of you and your surliness. I've been keeping you around out of habit, but this is the last straw. Your loyalty does not excuse this affront!" She straightened her wrap and smoothed back her hair which still looked perfect.

Marlin stepped back, embarrassed at his outburst. It wasn't his place, but he had to say something. He just couldn't bear it anymore.

"Fine. No orphans tonight," Fiana said as she opened her clutch and pulled out her lipstick. Regarding herself in the window, she freshened up. "But you will be punished for crossing me." She put her lipstick back in her clutch, snapped it shut with resolution, and looked at Marlin square in the eyes. "I've been slumming it with you for far too long. I think it's high time for a replacement."

A chill ran down Marlin's back. No words came to him. This statement was so unbelievable and shocking, that his mind was a complete blank.

In the silence following her declaration, faint sounds of sobbing could be heard from a nearby alley. Fiana, always happy to revel in the suffering of others, strode off towards the weeping and turned down the alleyway.

Amidst the stench and piled trash, a man squatted like a frog, crying uncontrollably. His dirty, tear-streaked face looked up into Fiana's as she approached, but he seemed to look right through her in a hysterical daze.

"She was alive. My wife! They buried her alive. Oh my God, they buried her alive," the voice said in a whimper. He looked away and buried his face in his hands. "My kids. They're all gone. My life is over."

"Are you okay?" Fiana said gently, "please, sir, let us help you." She reached down and touched his arm causing the man to jump.

Moody, who had followed her into the alley, tried to shrink inside the wall. He knew what was coming. This was fun for her.

The young man looked up at her.

"He'll do just fine," she said with a sideways glance at Moody.

Marlin cowered against the brick wall and whimpered. She wouldn't really do it. She wouldn't replace him. Not after all his years of service. She's just angry, that's all. Tomorrow everything will be back to normal.

"Do you want to die?" Fiana asked the man, smiling.

The usual horror followed by the resounding *NO* and pathetic begging to stave off the inevitable didn't come this time. The man looked at her seriously and said one word:

"Yes."

This surprised Fiana. She couldn't say it was unprecedented, but normally people—all creatures—wanted to live.

"You do?"

"If it will end this pain; knowing she died alone, clawing at the inside of her coffin lid like a trapped beast. I welcome death. There is nothing here for me now. There is nothing but death. And my poor Ruth, gone. Suffocated. How could they make such a mistake?" The wailing began again. "How could they make such a mistake and bury her alive?"

"They buried your wife alive?" Fiana said with laughter in her voice.

Moody was horrified at what he heard next, but Fiana reveled in it.

"There were too many sick, and my Ruth was but another. I had to go back to my children who had already started showing symptoms. I thought she was dead, my Ruth. I thought she was dead and so did the doctor. I went back to care for the children, but they died that night. It had only been a day. Only a day and they were dead. My little ones! My Ruth!" he wailed.

"The doctor took their little bodies down to where my Ruth was. They would all be buried together. I couldn't feel a thing. Numb. I told him I wanted to see my Ruth one last time. Just one last time. He had already put her in a coffin and sealed it up tight. He said it helped stop the spread of the flu, but when he opened the lid—oh God! The look on her face. Her bloodied hands!" More wailing.

"Well, now that that's off your chest. Let's get down to business," Fiana said, but this broken man didn't hear her over his blubbering. She tried not to smile, but she couldn't hide the smile in her eyes. It lit up the entire alley. Even Moody could see it from where he hid in the shadows. She was truly enjoying this.

The man was so distraught he didn't notice or didn't care.

"Enough," Moody cried from the wall, "please, no more!" Tears streamed down his face. He couldn't take anymore pain. She had become more ruthless as the years went by, and he just couldn't take it anymore. All these poor people living out the horror of this epidemic. It was bad enough without her enjoying it so.

Fiana ignored him as if he wasn't there.

The weeping man stood up before her. He was taller than her and not bad on the eyes, beneath all the tears.

"Hello tall, dark, and tragic," she said, "So you want to die? This is your lucky night mister."

"Death is all that's left for me," he replied, clearly unaware of what he was saying. His eyes stared off into the undefined distance. Unfocused. Unseeing.

"Oh yes, he'll do just fine," Fiana said to no one in particular, biting her lower lip seductively, "This is certainly something I can sink my teeth into."

"No," Moody whimpered from behind her.

Fiana whipped her head around in annoyance. "Do shut up, Moody! This is just business as usual. Enough of your constant whining! I meant what I said. Go away! You bore me!"

Moody stood there in shock. His eyes widened with the understanding of what she said. She wouldn't do it. She couldn't. Surely, she couldn't.

"I said go," Fiana said as she turned back to her prey, "Now, let's get this show on the road." She moved in closely to the broken man, laying her hand on his shoulder. This seemed to wrest the man from his catatonia, and he seemed to see her for the first time. Looking deeply into his eyes and slinking against him, she said, "What do they call you, sir?"

"James," he replied. Now his eyes, almost glazed over, transfixed, focused solely on her.

"Well, James, welcome to the family," she whispered in his ear.

"No!" Moody shrieked, as he heard her fangs pierce skin. She had to stand on her tip toes to reach James's neck at first, but as he weakened from the loss of blood, it was easier for her to reach and drink her fill. She clasped his body tightly to hers, draining him.

The smell of fresh blood mixed with the scent of death that lingered everywhere in the city. Moody never had gotten used to the stench of blood, not in all these years. It still made him a little queasy.

James dropped to the ground as Fiana released her grasp and pulled away. He was still breathing, very slightly—but still breathing.

Moody watched in horror as she knelt before him and removed the hat pin from her hat. She wasn't going to kill him; she was going to turn him! Was this poor man his replacement?

Fiana punctured her wrist with the sharp pin and then ripped a small opening in her vein to make the blood flow more freely. She put her dripping wrist up to the mouth of the dying man, but he turned away. Unlike most of her victims, this man didn't even shudder at the thought of death. He truly wanted to die. He accepted the sight of her in her true form without flinching. He didn't scream or beg. There wasn't even any fear in his eyes. The nightmare he had sustained over the past few days far outweighed facing death at the teeth of a vampire, but Fiana wouldn't give up. Once she knew what she wanted, there was no stopping her. She milked her arm to help the blood flow and let it drip down into his open, dying mouth.

"You will be mine," she whispered. "You are far too pretty and tragic to die tonight. Well, you'll die all right, but you'll be reborn."

The blood dripped onto James's lips, and he unconsciously licked it off.

The survival instinct always kicks in.

"Won't we look glamorous together out on the town, in whichever town we choose? Certainly better arm candy than dumpy old Moody," she said with a cruel sideways glance at Moody.

James grabbed onto her wrist and held it tightly to his mouth, sucking deeply.

She smiled and let him drink.

"Lady, please," Moody whispered from the sidelines. He was no longer crying. It had become far too serious for tears.

"Are you still here?" she replied coldly.

"I am always here, you know that," Moody said.

"Yes. That's the problem. Leave now before I lose my temper."

She pulled her arm free from the hungry mouth. James began writhing on the ground as the change took him over. First came the death, and it wasn't a peaceful death. James's woeful wails that filled the alleyway so recently had transformed into screams of pain. James curled up tight into a little fetal ball, as if it would stop the agony of death. Fiana remembered this pain. It had been over a millennia, but she remembered it as if it were only a few years ago. One doesn't forget this kind of pain. Ever. It's the pain of death and the pain of birth all wrapped into a huge mass of glorious agony. Indescribable, succulent agony.

Fiana watched with a patient smile as her new creation was born anew.

"You'll change your mind," Moody said, interrupting her maternal experience. "I have always been there for you, through it all. You won't cast me aside."

"Watch me."

"But, my lady."

Fiana wheeled around in a blur and was upon Moody before he could react. Her face was pure fury and her eyes completely black. She pinned him against the wall. Although she was much smaller than him in size, her strength far exceeded his. She spoke slowly and without emotion or anger, which told Marlin that her anger had surpassed even rage. "Leave. Now. Or you will not live to see another day. Leave. Now."

She let him go and turned back to her new companion. The screams now only a faint whimper. She knelt before him and wiped the remaining mortal sweat from his new stony brow.

"Good Morning," she said.

With that Moody turned and walked away, leaving Fiana with her new pet. Surely she would forget all about it by tomorrow. He spent the rest of the long, lonely night in silence walking up and down the quiet streets contemplating the unexpected turn of events. It was nearing dawn, so he must return and help his lady to sleep. He needed the rest, too. Upon arriving at their building, the door was locked and he remembered she always kept the key. He tried to unlock it with a wave of his hand, but it wouldn't budge. She had locked him out, physically and magically.

It's just part of the punishment, that's all, he reassured himself and sat down on the cold sidewalk as the sun began to rise. His heart felt hollow with her rejection. He knew there was no sense in beating on the door, as she was already sound asleep. He would just wait around until sunset, and then they would make amends. All would be well again after sunset. Moody settled back against the brick wall and slept.

The day came and went. Few people were out due to the epidemic, so he had a fairly uninterrupted sleep for most of the day.

When Fiana emerged that evening with her new companion, she acted as if Moody wasn't even there. She did not appear to hear his protests or apologies. She didn't see him following her all night from place to place. For Moody, it was even more disturbing to watch her work from the sidelines, especially with her new companion. They killed indiscriminately.

James was a quick and enthusiastic study.

They also did visit the orphanage together. Moody tried to keep enough distance not to hear the children scream, but he didn't stay far enough away.

The next few weeks passed in a blur of sleepless days and following Fiana at night. He sat on her doorstep, and it reminded him of Caedmon all those centuries ago. Would he turn into a dog again? He felt like a homeless mutt left hungry on the cold streets. But the loss of her love was the coldest of all. The time on the streets hadn't been kind to him. He was dirty, still wearing the same three-piece suit and fedora as their last night out together. Although the fedora no longer looked as smart and the suit was filthy and torn in places. He had tried to use his magic to keep warm, but his powers failed him. His grief consumed him, as he had nothing in this world anymore. His brothers were dead. His lady cast him aside. He had no one. Now in his depression, his magic failed him, too. Since Fiana had always taken care of them both, he had no money, save a few dollars which he used to eat sparingly. He pawned his pocket watch for a few more meals, but that was all he had.

Then one night everything changed for several reasons.

First, it would be his last on this doorstep, but not for the reason he had been hoping for. Fiana emerged with James as she did every night, dressed to the nines and looking gorgeous.

James looked very handsome in a tux, and he seemed to be adjusting very well to his new life.

This time was different because this time when Moody begged at her feet for forgiveness, she actually looked at him while he pleaded, "Please, Fiana—I have nothing, no money, nowhere to go. My life has all been for you. It's all for you."

She stared at him coldly for a moment before responding, "You're a big boy, and I'm sure you can take care of yourself. I do not want to see you again. The next time I see your face, I will kill you." Fiana showed no pity, no anger, no emotion at all on her marble face.

Moody was rendered speechless. He looked up at her and knew the truth of her words. Tears blurred his vision and his jaw began to tremble.

"Here," Fiana said reaching into her clutch, "get yourself cleaned up and then disappear from my sight. Start a new life somewhere else or forfeit yours." She threw some crumpled bills at his feet and strode away.

Moody picked up the money and smoothed them out. His lady could be quite generous. There was over one thousand dollars in his hands. He stood up as a tear streamed down his face. Although it was a lot of money, it wouldn't last too long; and he must keep close to her in case she needed him. He would be invisible to her, invisible to the world; but he would stay close. Perhaps she would fall on hard times and need him. He would be ready for that. His belly spoke to him, and he decided to keep a C-note to get a hot meal tonight and to eat sparingly for as long as it would last him. His trousers sagged from the lack of food over the past month, and he knew that he would eventually spend all this money just on food if he kept it with him.

He decided he would put it somewhere safe, invest it perhaps, then he would be ready for when she needed him. But how? He couldn't put it in a bank, as he legally did not exist. He began walking down the street until he came to a place with food. Taped in the widow was a red, white, and blue poster of an arm lighting a candle. The caption read: *Make this the Glorious 4th.*

"That's it!" he said to no one and disappeared into the night.

CHAPTER ELEVEN

January had arrived cold and frozen. It left swept away by wind and rain. Cullen was enjoying a respite. The past few weeks had been rather nice. No one mentioned Rowan or the forthcoming plan again. Cullen felt relieved. They finally got the message that he just did not want to talk about it.

Tomorrow was Imbolc, and Cullen still hadn't spoken to Rowan. He had tried, sort of, but he hadn't tried that hard. He liked having his body and mind to himself again, and he wasn't too anxious to have it taken over by the wizard. It was like being the alter-ego of a super hero without ever being the hero.

His feeling of peace ended at lunch. It started with Maddy and April nagging him.

"What do you mean you haven't talked to him yet?" Maddy said, "The ritual is tonight. I've been busy preparing all month, and you haven't even told the wizard!"

"I tried," Cullen said quietly, hoping Maddy would take the hint since other kids looked over at the word "wizard."

"You tried? He lives in your head, Cullen! How hard can it be to think to him?"

She didn't take the hint.

"It doesn't work like that," he said even more quietly than before.

"You told me it did," April said. The disappointment on her face and her calm tone were harder to take than Maddy's scolding.

"Well, it does sometimes, but now he's buried deep. It's not as easy as just thinking to him when he's hiding like this."

"I'm telling Ms. MacFey," Maddy threatened, huffily folding her arms.

"No. I'll do it now."

They both stared at him blankly. Maddy, with her arms crossed, tilted her head and raised her eyebrows waiting expectingly. April's gaze was actually not directly at him, but more over his right shoulder. She was really good at estimating where someone was, but she never got it just right.

Cullen closed his eyes, blocking out their apparent disappointment and concentrated.

Rowan? he thought, *ROWAN WAKE UP!*

This was just giving him a headache. The wizard was nowhere to be found in there.

"He's not answering," Cullen told the girls.

"That's it. I'm telling Ms. MacFey," Maddy said standing up abruptly and storming off toward the teacher's table.

"Wait for me!" April said to Cullen as he stood up to follow. She held out her hand towards him. He took it and felt his face flush. She moved her hand to his elbow and they took off together.

Only Ms. MacFey and Mr. Ferguson were at the teacher's table. Lunch period was almost over, so most of the teachers were already gone. They were standing up as if they were about to leave. Ms. MacFey had a sympathetic look on her face, while Mr. Ferguson looked embarrassed as they approached. She was touching his shoulder and Cullen heard her say, "I just don't think it's a good idea, Ralph. We work together."

Ms. MacFey turned to the kids, dropping her hand from Mr. Ferguson's shoulder and putting a smile on her face immediately after seeing them.

"Hi kids."

"Cullen hasn't spoken to Rowan yet about tonight!" Maddy blurted out.

Mr. Ferguson just stood there with a look of shock for a moment, but he seemed to regain his bearings and said, "Well, Ms. MacFey, I'll leave you to it. Kids." He began to turn and back away when a voice cracking with frustration shouted from the other end of the cafeteria loud enough to be heard over all the students talking.

"EVERYBODY FREEZE!"

As Cullen turned around to see who was shouting, a girl screamed.

Another shouted, "He's got a gun!"

Cullen couldn't even process what he saw before something pulled him backwards, and he crashed to the floor with a grunt of pain. He was behind an overturned table now with Ms. MacFey, Mr. Ferguson, Maddy, and April. They all looked frantic.

"Just stay still," Mr. Ferguson said, "It will all be over soon. I'm sure someone has called the police."

"I'm calling now," Ms. MacFey said as she dialed her iPhone.

"What's going on?" April asked.

"It's Fred," Maddy said, her voice shaking, "that frickin' idiot Fred."

"He's got a gun," Mr. Ferguson explained. Beads of sweat lined his furrowed forehead. "Just sit here quietly, and it will all be over soon."

"He's what!" Cullen said. His breath came faster and he swallowed hard. He felt Rowan peek out from inside. "No!" he screamed aloud to himself. He tried to get angry. He knew if he could control his fear he would stay in control of his body as well. He must control his fear. He began taking deep, controlled breaths. That's all he could hear, his breath. The screams and background noise faded away, and he breathed.

The POP! POP! broke his induced calm and the screams flooded back into his consciousness. He looked to his right at Mr. Ferguson with his back to the table's underside. His arms were wrapped around his knees and his eyes were shut tight. To his left, Ms. MacFey was on the phone still, holding a finger in one ear as she spoke in hushed tones, and Maddy and April had their arms around each other. Their eyes shut tight. He risked a quick peak over the top of the table. He saw Fred with the gun pointed at his own head, then at Principal Blake, then out at no one in particular, and then back at his own head. He didn't see any blood, so the two shots must've been in the air. Principal Blake stood in a defensive stance about five feet from him with her arms outstretched. She seemed to be coaxing him, trying to calm him. Fred's face, a contortion of rage and fear, was stained with tears. Just as the entire scene registered in Cullen's mind, Fred looked directly into his eyes and pointed the gun straight at Cullen's head.

"No!" This time it wasn't Cullen that screamed, but rather a voice inside his head.

Mr. Ferguson pulled him back down, but it was too late. He could hear Fred yelling and knew what was coming.

"I see you Knight. You don't deserve him. You stupid dweeb! You don't deserve him!" Fred said over and over.

What was he talking about? What could I possibly have that he'd be envious of? Cullen thought frantically. *Did he mean Rowan?*

Cullen's chest ached, stopping his thoughts. Pain. Then light burst out from his chest. His expanding body pushed against Mr. Ferguson's protective arm, and the last thing Cullen saw was a look of horror on Mr. Ferguson's face. The teacher scrambled desperately away, suddenly more afraid of Cullen than the gun.

Rowan stood up from behind the table and faced the angry boy coming at him. Something stung his shoulder causing him to stumble backward. Looking down, he saw the blood stain his green robe as it spread down toward his chest. He was obviously confronting a powerful weapon.

"You!" screamed the boy holding the strange smoking metal thing.

Recognition came to Rowan. This was one of the boys he had turned into a mouse when they had attacked April a few months ago. Rowan had but a moment to react before that metal thing barked at him again.

"*Stadaim!*" Rowan said with a flick of his wand, just as the boy fired.

Fred's face was frozen in a cry of rage. A small piece of pointed metal hung suspended in midair halfway between the angry boy and Rowan's chest.

"Rowan!" Ms. MacFey said standing up beside him. She threw her arms around his neck and pressed closely against him. "Thank God you're here!"

Rowan gently pushed her from him and hurried toward the door. He felt what she wanted from him, something he couldn't give. This was all too confusing. He must get out of this strange place. Nothing else mattered.

Many eyes peered out from behind overturned tables to see if it was safe as he left the cafeteria.

Max caught up with him in the hallway, grabbed his arm, and spun him around. Behind them, questions exploded from dozens of throats creating a cacophonous maelstrom.

"We have to get you out of here," she said. "The police will be here any minute, and we don't want to explain this. Can you do something about him?" She pointed to the still-frozen boy through the doorway. Students and teachers were cautiously approaching him, whispering to each other. Principal Blake checked behind every table for injuries, but apparently found none.

With a lazy wave of his wand and a softly spoken "*dul a chodladh*," the statuesque boy at the far end of the cafeteria fell to the floor just as a football player heroically tackled him. The suspended bullet found a home in the wall behind the stage. A collective gasp replaced the whispers. Then cheers as they heralded the football player as the hero. It would be much easier to explain that story anyway.

Fred lay asleep on the floor.

Rowan turned once again to leave. Max was close behind saying something to him, but he wasn't listening.

The pain from his shoulder screamed at him. The loss of blood which now soaked the front of his robe weakened him. He fell against the metal lockers. More metal. More concrete. He hated this world. Then new, horrible, piercing wails filled the air. He clamped his hands over his ears and thought he must be in the hell that the Christians had warned him about.

Max knelt before him, put her hand on his good shoulder, and said, "The sirens. They're here. We have to get you out of here now. Please, come with me."

Rowan got up and let her lead him out the back door. She helped him stumble into the cover of the redwoods. He felt immediately better once surrounded by living wood, but the hole in his shoulder still hurt.

"What did this to me?" Rowan asked.

"It was a gun."

"A gun?"

Max tried to explain. "It's a weapon, and it lets people hurt other people from a distance. It propels a small piece of metal into another person. That's what happened to your shoulder." Her hand hovered above the wound wanting to soothe him, but afraid of hurting him more.

"It is like an arrow without a shaft?" Rowan asked.

"Sort of," Max replied.

"This weapon was made to kill people?"

"Yes."

Rowan placed his strong hand against the trunk of a huge tree and closed his eyes. Breathing deeply, he drew power from the ancient tree, up through its roots from the earth. The little metal piece pushed back out of his shoulder fell onto the forest floor as the wound closed. Rowan bent over to pick it up.

"This? This tiny thing did all that damage?"

"That was amazing," Max said in wonder, she reached out and touched his shoulder gently. "They can't send you away. We need you here."

He had no idea what she was talking about, but it made him angry. Cullen's anger stirred inside him, too. He grabbed Max and pulled her to him roughly.

"What do you mean 'send me away'?" he asked directly into her face, which was but inches from his own.

Max's frightened look softened and she reached for his lips with her own.

Before Rowan realized what she was doing, she kissed him. He had never been kissed by anyone but his wife. In that short moment, he tasted Max and it stirred something inside him. Cullen screamed, and Rowan pushed Max away just as roughly as he had grabbed her. Cullen was struggling for control of their body, but Rowan was not yet ready to give it up.

He pushed Cullen back down.

What did this woman mean when she said "send him away?" Now she was kissing him, and it brought back all the pain of Fiana's betrayal that still burned so deeply in his chest. Something between anger and pain lingered there like a heavy weight. It filled his heart like hot liquid. He fought back the tears. He could feel his heart beating hard, deep within. He looked down at his chest to see the skin and muscle moving in time with his broken heartbeat. At least when he was out, he didn't have to protect Cullen from his experience of pain. Spending so much time inside Cullen's mind, he knew that to feel what the dominant felt took concentration. When inside, he could hide deep and not feel anything. Out here he could just be and feel without worrying about protecting anyone else.

In the sanctuary of the forest, he let the grief wash over him. The loss of his entire way of life. His wife. His people. His world. The pain from such a loss still burned as if it had only been a few months, which for him, it had. This forest was his world, surrounded by life, but this was not his time. Had he been truly a part of the world today, he would already know that things like friendship and trust no longer meant what they once did. Things were much simpler in his time—much more honest and real, full of life and love. Simpler, but deeper, like the roots of the trees extending deep into the earth. But now the forests were disappearing. Now there was too much metal and concrete and glass. It had made people hard. It had made them shallow. He remembered what he saw in San Francisco, everyone rushing around going nowhere. Empty inside. Filling their bodies with distilled spirits and other alchemical poisons just to make it through the next day. All reeling towards death unaware. A waste of life.

And now this! This horrible black machine created for no other apparent purpose than to take away life, as if death did not come soon enough.

He regained control of his emotions and turned back to Max, who had kept a little distance from him since he had been so rough with her. Tears gleamed in her eyes.

"I will ask you again, woman. What do you mean 'send me away'?"

"Tonight, you are to cross over into the Otherworld and remain there while Cullen returns to this world."

"Is it Samhain again?" Rowan asked in disbelief. Had he lost all sense of time?

"No, it is Imbolc."

"But the veil does not open on Imbolc."

"Marlin believes that you and he can force it open on this feast day with your combined magics."

"And Cullen wants this?"

Max didn't say anything, but looked at the ground.

"Of course he does," Rowan said to himself. Cullen had made that perfectly clear. He was, after all, an unwanted squatter in the boy's body and a danger to him as well. It was for the best. He knew that.

"I don't want it," Max offered, looking back up at him.

"What do you want, woman? Do you think we can be together? Do you think you can love me? I live inside a little boy! I am from another time and I am married—to a vampire," he said the last with a millennium of regret. Fiana. A vampire. He could still scarcely believe it. And it was all because she was trying to find him, a coward who had hidden in the face of danger rather than face it like a man. Now all was lost. All had been lost for centuries, but for him the wound was still gaping and raw. This wound could not be healed with energy borrowed from the earth.

"You're right, of course," Max said, pulling him out of his self-pity. "It is crazy, Rowan, but I can't control what I feel for you. And I don't want you to go into the Otherworld never to

109

return. We need you here! What would've happened today if you hadn't been here?"

"Perhaps it is for the best," Rowan said with a sigh. He sat down at the base of a redwood and rested his arms on the tops of his knees. The breeze caught his hair and blew it across his face, tangling it with his beard. He looked away from Max.

She knelt next to him and brushed the long red locks away from his face tenderly.

"Rowan, we need you here. I need you here."

Rowan looked back at Max and saw the love on her face. He recognized it because he had seen Fiana look at him that way for so long. But behind the love, he saw the fear and the knowledge that they could not be together.

"Perhaps it is for the best," Rowan repeated, stopping her hand on his jaw with his own and gently pulling it down. "I have caused too much trouble here already. Cullen will be here in a moment, for he is trying to come back out. I have kept him pushed down, but it is not my place to do so. Please tell him that I will go into the Otherworld tonight and remain there. I will stay hidden until then. He can have his body back, and mind, too."

Rowan resigned himself to his fate, a long overdue fate. Looking back at the school with all the people milling around and flashing lights, he said, "I am not of this world. I do not understand it with all the death and destruction, and I do not care to understand it."

Rowan took Max's hand and kissed it gently, holding it for a moment longer. "My time is past, and I must face the fate I should have endured centuries ago." He placed her hand on the ground and patted it.

She looked down at her hand, where his had so recently been. When she looked back up again, Cullen sat before her, fuming.

CHAPTER TWELVE

Rowan brushed her cheek gently with the back of his hand, and Fiana smiled, blushing. She looked up at his strong face, smiling down back at her. It was their wedding night, finally. After decades of waiting and studying the Druidic ways side by side, the night had finally come. She felt nervous, but more thrilled than anything else. The cold November wind wildly blew his red locks until they entwined with hers. He took her by the waist and pulled her close to him. Intense desire mixed with tender love flared in his eyes. They had waited so long. So very, very long. Fiana stood wrapped in the arms of Rowan while the tall heather in full bloom surrounding them danced with the Highland winds. Her head rested against his powerful chest. The cadence of his heart played the bass beat of her life's song. They were together, and that was all that mattered.

She tilted her head upwards asking for a kiss. He gladly obliged, tasting her love with eager tenderness. She met his kiss with a lifetime of desire. He held her tightly to him, his strong arms around her waist. She felt as if she would melt into him. Pressing more closely against him, she drank him in.

Then she was alone.

She spun around looking for her husband and called out his name, but there was no answer. Her solitary voice echoed across the empty Highlands. Then silence.

A faint scraping sound broke the quiet. It was the Bean Nighe. The Washerwoman. Portent of death. Her webbed feet gripped the stones in the stream, and her hands raked something across the rocks. Fiana, couldn't help but move closer. Horrified, she screamed. The washerwoman did not pause, but continued scrubbing blood out of Rowan's wedding robe.

Fiana gasped and collapsed into an airless lump as she felt Rowan emerge and rip her from her dream. She awoke in total darkness, on the floor of her darkened bedchamber.

How had she gotten to the floor? She looked up at her bed. Empty.

She wept silently, alone on the floor in her room. After fourteen centuries, his touch felt so real. Their love so strong and pure. But it was just a dream. That same dream. Their dream, that had turned into a nightmare.

It had been a little over two months, a mere blink in time for one as old as she, but these past months had felt like an eternity even to her. That's when this blasted dream returned. After centuries, she had found him at last, and lost him again. It was more than she could bear. Up until that Samhain night, she had finally believed that the entire business was just a fairy tale she had convinced herself was true. Then she felt him emerge last Samhain, and her long lifetime of pain and sacrifice filled her up again.

There must be a way to stop this! She worked too hard, too long to be crippled by love again. But even more than the feeling of love, the sensation of their spiritual connection was causing her to feel almost alive again. It was seductively sweet and unbearably painful all at once. She was being torn apart by emotions she shouldn't be feeling. Not now. Not after all she had given up. What was a vampire witch to do?

Ever since she had been forced away from Rowan by her former servant Moody Marlin and that wretched woman teacher in the redwood forest last November, she had been plotting her revenge. How dare they come between her and her husband? Who did they think they were? Especially that woman! How dare that woman come between them! It was adding insult to injury watching her hold him as she was cast aside like a used tissue. And Rowan. He looked so broken, so frightened of her. Of her! His wife! She had never meant to hurt him, not really. She was just used to getting her way is all. That's all it was, persuasion. He was the one being difficult. He knew they were meant to be together. Why was he fighting it?

"Stop it!" she admonished herself aloud. She braced herself against the windowsill and stood back up, smoothing out her green satin nightgown.

It's so silly to get all worked up. After all, it has been over a thousand years!

Shaking off the realness of her recent dream, she gathered her wits.

Why should she care what he thinks or feels after all this time? He was the one who had abandoned her! It was because of him that she lived for so many cold years wandering the earth in search of him. Using all her magic to stay alive, healthy, and young to find him and release him from that wretched wand.

She snatched her matching satin robe from the hook by the closet, put it on, and cinched the tie tightly around her slender waist.

It was because of him she sacrificed her soul when magic could no longer sustain her. It was all for him.

She regarded herself in the mirror, thankful that it was only a myth about vampires and mirrors. She looked good. And not only good for a fourteen-hundred-year-old vampire. She looked good, period. Porcelain skin. Cat-green eyes. Naturally curly, flaming red hair. She merely needed to fluff it up with her fingers after sleeping. No styling necessary. She was as gorgeous as ever. Much more beautiful than that plain school teacher. There was just no comparison. Yes. She looked good, hadn't aged a day since her wedding day. She looked like a perfectly preserved forty-year-old woman. Not young enough to look like a child, not old enough to look like a crone. Just a hint of creasing around her eyes and mouth, showing her having lived a life of happiness in the Highlands with Rowan. None of the grief that followed her wedding day showed on her face. None of the loss or regret or sacrifice showed on her pearly skin. She had been preserved, in outward appearance at least, as the happy woman she was on her wedding day fourteen-hundred years ago. The only difference was the single strand of white hair down the right side and a single lock of black down the left.

She was captured in the beautiful prime of her womanhood.

Rowan, too, had not aged a day. He looked as handsome as the day they were married. Somewhere deep in her memory she coaxed forth the way she shivered when he'd touch her cheek and how she would gasp for breath when she'd catch him watching her out on the Highlands all those centuries ago. When she really concentrated, it seemed like it was only yesterday. The recurring dream also helped keep it fresh. Too fresh.

"Pull yourself together, woman," she sneered at herself.

She stood up proud, determined to let that be the last time he affected her in that way. She curled the single lock of white and black framing her face around each finger.

She must control him.

She must have him.

She must consume him.

She drew back the heavy black curtains and looked out the stone-lined window over the bay. She kept her distance from the window as the sun was still out. Rowan surfacing jarred her from her daytime slumber. She rarely saw the daylight, and she liked to see the world bathed in light sometimes, although it was all much more beautiful at night. The water normally looked black, but in the sunlight it almost looked blue. The trees were a brilliant green, like the color of her eyes. She didn't much like the forest anymore, though. She saw the Green Man's face in every tree and it mocked her sorrow. It mocked her failure. But overall, she really loved this island. It provided her with the privacy her lifestyle often required.

She had purchased this tiny, private island decades ago. A formality really, since she had already owned it in a more primal reality. It lies somewhere between Seattle and Victoria off the Orca Islands southern coast. It proved to be a perfect fortress, a getaway for when she needed some time to herself. No one ever came out there, except for the random group of kids chancing their fate against the old lore about the place. Passersby had heard screams on occasion. Despite the tales they told each other, most believed it was only the wind among the rocks, and sometimes that's all they were.

She smiled at the thought.

Rumors started. They always did. Leave it to the humans to make up tall tales around the things that go bump in the night. Of course, the reality was much more deliciously horrible than their small minds imagined. Few kids actually made it out there, as no commercial ferries traveled to that island. One would either need a private boat or a commissioned one. Both options were quite pricey just to investigate ghost stories. The official story, of course, was that it was owned by an old, recluse heiress who didn't like the company of others. She would prosecute any trespassers, it was told.

That was one way to put it.

"My Lady, are you awake?" James's voice spoke from outside her chamber door, interrupting her thoughts.

"I am," she responded dryly. She hated having her ruminations intruded upon.

"I thought I heard you fall. Is everything all right?"

"Everything is fine, James. Now go away."

"It's him isn't it?"

Her thoughts jolted back to Rowan and the dream. Her heart filled with grief. Damn James for this. She had been having such pleasant thoughts of the frightened peons. Now her mind and heart were once again filled with Rowan. Damn them both.

"Yes. It's him," she said through the door, rubbing her temples.

"Don't worry, Lady, we'll find him, or if you wish, we can bring him to us."

Fiana opened the door to find James standing there smiling and already dressed in his favorite: black leather, with his black hair pulled back into a single black ribbon. There was a definite gleam in his brilliant blue eyes, and he had a puckish look about him. It made her smile, draining all the sorrow from her eyes. They became childlike and playful.

"Oooh—you have a plan, don't you?"

"I do."

"Is it deliciously wicked?"

"Of course. And it will satisfy us both." He took her hand in a very formal way and led her from her chamber to the stairs. Fiana's long green satin robe trailed behind her.

She did look good in green.

"Do tell!" Fiana said as he led them down the spiral staircase of their Castle-House. That's what she liked to call it, for it was built like a modern castle, accented with Tudor-style decor around the windows. The reign of the Tudors had been her favorite age. It had been so lusciously bloody with all those beheadings and burnings, although she had a small spot of solicitude for those who were burned alive. She had come too close for comfort to that fate herself. It's what had finally made her drop her pointless quest and embrace her new identity. It had been a good time to be bloodthirsty. She liked the reminder of the good ol' days in her architecture.

"It requires bait."

Fiana liked the sound of this already. "What sort of bait?"

"Can't you think of anyone who would be perfect bait for your dear Rowan?"

As they reached the first floor, one corner of Fiana's lips rose in a crooked smile.

"That *woman*."

"Yes, *that* woman." James smiled. Taking her nacreous hands into his own. "Let me go back to Fortuna, my queen. Let me finish what I started there. I didn't like being interrupted during my snack. Not at all."

Hateful happiness spread warmly through Fiana's body like fresh blood on a winter's night.

"Yes, I'd like her gone, too. She cares for Rowan far too much for my tastes."

"She's with him now, you know," James said, toying with her dangerously.

Fiana winced.

James noticed and pressed his luck by continuing, "Is it a coincidence he emerged for Imbolc? Perhaps he desires love anew."

Fiana reacted quickly and without mercy. Her hand flew to James's throat and pinned him to the wall. If he had breath, she'd have cut it off with her strength. Fury burned in her eyes, but James just laughed (as well as he could through her tight grasp). This infuriated her more. "How dare you suggest that my husband desires another woman!"

"Don't worry. We'll get her. She won't touch him ever again," he said in a breathy whisper, for Fiana's grip kept his vocal cords from vibrating.

"Promise?" Her grip tightened.

"Promise," he squeaked.

Fiana released him.

He dropped with a loud thud as his leather boots hit the wooden floor. He steadied himself against the wall and stood proudly before her, rubbing the red marks from his neck.

Fiana patted his cheek a little too hard before turning away with a smile. Looking back at him over her shoulder, she said with sudden understanding, "*You* want her, don't you?"

"Her blood was intoxicating! A hint of Fey, if I'm not mistaken. I want more." He licked his lips at the memory of it and swallowed hard. He rushed up to her side and continued, "There is power there, and it's ours for the taking. Plus, it will bring Rowan directly to you."

"I'm glad to see you're motivated, James. It has been so long since you were passionate about anything. But we must plan carefully. He must be mine again, forever."

A vampire dressed in a tux entered the room with a fresh glass of blood on a tray. He bowed slightly and clicked his heels together, offering it to her. She took it and absentmindedly waved her hand to dismiss him. All of her lower servants were perfectly trained in Victorian etiquette. They also did things in the exact way she wanted them, or they knew what could happen to them. They had seen it happen. So the utmost care was taken when preparing any of Fiana's food. Blood had to be at a perfect 98.6 degrees when she took her first sip.

As she drank her breakfast, her mind began racing with ideas and schemes. A drop of blood ran down the outside of the chalice; she caught it with her finger as she looked at the whale-shaped talisman locked inside a glass case. It reminded her of Rowan's wand in more ways than one. Licking the rescued morsel off her finger, she began to daydream what she and Rowan would do together once she had him there. Her face flushed with the heat she had felt in the recent dream.

But there was that little boy.

That cooled her down. She took another sip of breakfast.

That little boy was always around, and if he saw James take the teacher then Rowan would emerge and stop him. Everything would be ruined.

"The boy," she began.

"Yes. The boy cannot see or Rowan will emerge and ruin everything like he did the last time," James said, as if reading her mind. "That was unfortunate. But worry not, my sweet. I will wait until the proper moment, when there are some helpless witnesses. The right ones. Ones that will draw Rowan here. And draw him here alone."

"Nice thinking, James. Just be sure to bring her back alive. We must get him here thinking he can save her. That hero stuff appeals to him. Always did."

"Oh yes, she'll be a lot of fun alive." James smiled, greatly amused at the thought of getting Max back under his control.

CHAPTER THIRTEEN

Cullen went straight home from the forest. Ms. MacFey was concerned and wanted to talk. They always wanted to talk. He just wanted to be left alone. He didn't want to deal with the police or his friends and especially not Rowan. Cullen couldn't figure out how he felt about Rowan, let alone talk about all this. He thought of Rowan as a friend, of sorts, and he was certainly grateful for his help in an increasingly dangerous world, but he didn't want to be possessed either. He wanted Rowan out of his body and mind. If only there were some way for him to get his body back. Then they could both be happy.

Yeah, and why we're at it, we'll just cure Fiana of her vampirism, he thought cynically.

Trudy was sure to be angry at his early arrival, but he would rather deal with her than all the other stuff making a mess of his life. How could she really blame him after what happened today anyway. Knowing Trudy, she'd find a way. He was used to his foster mother's surliness, at least that's normal. As normal as his life gets these days. Frank and Rex probably wouldn't be home yet, so that was a small blessing. Let her be angry.

I'll yell back this time, he thought to himself. *I'll stand up for myself.*

But when he entered the house, she wasn't in her usual place, drunk on the couch. Just an empty bottle of vodka and "You Oughta Know" blasting from the stereo speakers. The song ended and then automatically started again. It must be set on repeat. Alanis Morrisette. Cullen knew that Trudy really wasn't in a good mood now. She had often referred to it as her "power music." It reminded her of her strength as a woman or something like that. He turned down the music and listened.

Nothing.

He started down the hall toward his bedroom, but he still heard nothing.

"Mrs. Samuels?" he called. Although Cullen had lived with the Samuels for over six years now, he still had to call them Mr. and Mrs. Samuels. Fine with him. What was the alternative? Mom? He would never call her that, even if he was allowed. "Mrs. Samuels?"

No response.

He walked further down the hall. A very horrid sound came from the Samuels' bedroom. A short, burst of retching.

Then it was quiet.

Cullen approached their almost-closed door and listened. He didn't hear anything else. He knocked lightly, as if he would be scolded for doing so. Of course, he probably would be. He wasn't allowed in their room.

"Mrs. Samuels?" he said quietly.

Nothing.

Upon entering the bedroom cautiously, he saw that the bathroom door was also nearly closed, but a light was on. He tapped lightly on the door. He was really pushing his luck! Not only was he home early, but he was also in their bedroom. Still, he felt that something wasn't right.

"Mrs. Samuels?"

He heard that grisly retching again and a weak voice say, "Go away."

Then the stench hit him. It was earthy and vile, and it made Cullen take a deep breath through his mouth and hold his nose shut for a moment. Something must be really wrong.

"Are you okay, Mrs. Samuels?" he said after unclenching his nose, but he still breathed through his mouth.

"No. I'm not okay." She sounded very sick and annoyed, but she wasn't yelling.

This was new.

Cullen tentatively went inside, expecting her wrath at any moment. He was still ready to meet it with his own in kind, but unwarranted sympathy was starting to replace his anger. What he saw washed all his hostility away.

Trudy had been crying.

In the six years he had lived there, he had never seen Trudy cry. In fact, he had never seen Trudy show any emotion except anger, annoyance, and pride in her son, Rex. And sometimes a gloating satisfaction when a respected member of the community suffered a humiliation.

But she had definitely been crying. Her mascara ran in long black streaks down her face. Her eyes were red and her face puffy. She was in bad shape, emotionally and physically. Sprawled on the bathroom floor, she hugged the toilet. The smell proved that it had been well-used already, and not just from throwing up. She wore a ratty bathrobe over her favorite house dress. It was old and worn and wet with vomit. She looked horrible.

Cullen noticed another empty bottle of vodka laying next to her bare legs. That was the second empty bottle. Surely she hadn't drunk all that vodka today!

No wonder she was sick.

"Um. Mrs. Samuels, are you okay?"

She tried to speak, but retched instead. There was nothing more to come out, but her body still tried to expel the poison.

"Can I do something to help you?" Cullen offered. He had no idea what to do.

"No one can help me. My life is nothing. It's nothing but a lie," she said quietly, like a broken person. "I just want to die."

New tears streamed down her face, cutting fresh lines through her streaked mascara. She kept her head down, looking into the toilet bowl, as if too ashamed to look at Cullen. Tears dripped off her small nose into the muck below.

"I haven't the strength to continue living this lie, Cullen," she said in a barely audible whisper.

Cullen didn't know what to say, so he didn't say anything. He just waited silently, watching her cry. The only sound was her continuous soft sobbing. He wanted to reach out to comfort her, but that was probably pushing his luck. He hated to see anything in pain, human or non-human—even Trudy.

Trudy broke the silence with a sickening gagging sound, as she tried to vomit again.

Cullen grimaced, covering his nose. He made sure Trudy didn't see him do it. No need to make her feel worse.

She obviously had nothing on her stomach. The vodka was already in her blood. She sat back against the side of the bathtub next to the toilet and covered her face. Her bathrobe fell off one shoulder, and Cullen noticed that her skin was all splotched in red across her chest and arm. Alcohol poisoning. He recognized it because of a report he had to do on it in school once. The administration was apparently trying to deter drinking at a young age. But who drinks at twelve? Rex probably had. Maybe Maddy does. But seeing this was all the information he needed to never drink.

Trudy whimpered and Cullen stooped down in front of her, gingerly reaching out to pat her shoulder. As he touched her, she jumped and looked up at him with wide eyes. She looked frightened and really tired. Her eyes, normally sunken, were rimmed in an even deeper darkness. It wasn't just from the mascara. She looked scared, too, as if she had forgotten he was there.

"Oh. You're still here," she said scowling, returning to her normal self momentarily. Then the stern angry look typically etched on her face melted away again, and Cullen saw the shattered woman beneath. She pulled her robe back up onto her shoulder and wrapped her arms around herself.

"It's been a lie. My entire life is a lie," she repeated in a cracked voice. Her lips looked blue.

"What do you mean?" Cullen asked gently.

She regarded him for a moment through half-closed eyes before saying, "My marriage. My pathetic life. It's over, Cullen. It's over before it even began. For Christ's sake, I'm only thirty-three, and my life is over! How could I have been such a fool?" Her eyes drooped, as if she was falling asleep for a heartbeat before popping back open. "Such a stupid fool." she continued. "Where did it all go so wrong?" She looked away from him, lowering her head. She stared at a tiny spot on her leg and started tracing it over and over and over with her fingers, making tiny invisible circles around the freckle.

"My life is just slipping away. Right before my eyes. Where has the last decade gone? I'll be forty before long, and then fifty. Sixty. Seventy. Eighty. Death. Death is inevitable, and I'm reeling towards death in mediocrity. Nothing to show for it. All for nothing."

Her words were getting softer and softer.

"All for nothing. I'm just going to get old and die anyway. Die. Just like my dreams. All dead. Gone."

Cullen, as usual, didn't know what to say, and that annoyed him. His annoyance then made him angry. Why did he have to deal with this, especially after what happened at school today. It's too much. It's all too much.

She continued her lament. "Do you have dreams?" Trudy interrupted his mounting anger, lifting her head up enough to look at him again. "Of course you do," she said before he could answer. "Of course you have dreams. Who doesn't?" The tears began to flow. "I don't. That's who. Not anymore. I'm tired of dreaming. I'm tired of being disappointed. I'm tired of feeling like a failure, of being married to a failure. Mediocrity. I always thought it would get better, that he'd become someone. That we'd become someone and be like we were." She heaved again and flung herself over the toilet just in time. Somehow, her body managed to produce some more sickly fluid.

Cullen had seen Trudy drunk, quite often, really, but he had never seen Trudy like this, not in his entire life. She was past broken. She was destroyed. What had happened? She and Frank had never been okay, not as long as he'd been here, but they seemed content at least; civil.

"He said he'd take me to Paris," she said as her eyes began to close again. "Where has he ever taken me? I'm nothing to him. Perhaps *she* means something to him. That Jezebel. I won't be second to anyone. I have my pride after all." Her words were becoming slurred. "To think, another son, too." Her words faded off towards the end.

What was she talking about? Another son? Had Frank been cheating on her? Did he have a mistress and a bastard son!

Cullen's surprise wasn't based on his low opinion of Frank's moral fiber. He just couldn't imagine who else would want him!

He remembered something Fred said to him just before Rowan had emerged this morning: "You don't deserve him."

Could he have meant Frank?

That was just too crazy.

"Just reeling towards death," Trudy mumbled, breaking into his thoughts. She slumped over the toilet, unconscious.

Cullen sympathized with her. He knew how it felt to be cast aside by Frank.

At least she's resting now. Maybe she can sleep it off, Cullen thought, but then he noticed the empty bottle of Vicodin that had fallen behind the toilet.

That's not good.

"Mrs. Samuels!" Cullen cried in alarm.

She didn't move.

"Mrs. Samuels!" he yelled, panic edging in his voice.

She still didn't move.

"TRUDY," he shouted, yanking her up. She remained unconscious. Her head lolled to the side like a rag doll's. Cullen had a hard time holding even the top half of her up. She was dead weight. He tried to lay her back down gently, but her head made a dull thud when it hit the bathroom floor.

Cullen stepped back, scared. Is she still breathing? Cullen watched closely to see the shallow rise and fall of her chest. She was still alive, but for how long? He didn't know what to do!

"9-1-1," he said aloud, "I've got to call 9-1-1."

The ambulance arrived shortly thereafter, but not soon enough for Cullen, who had to fret and pace beside the unconscious Trudy for what seemed like forever. She smelled bad and looked worse. He feared she would die, and he wouldn't know what to do if she did. Every few seconds he checked her pulse, just as the woman at 9-1-1 told him to do. He also had turned her on her side as instructed. He could see why, since she continued to retch and heave in her unconscious state. All that puke just dribbled out the side of her mouth onto the bathroom floor. He would have to clean that up before Frank got home.

Trudy was still unconscious when they put her in the ambulance.

"Will she be okay?" Cullen asked the EMT as he and his partner hooked Trudy up to all kinds of machines and put some kind of mask over her face. Probably oxygen.

"We'll do everything we can," the EMT said as he closed the ambulance doors.

That's not what I asked, Cullen thought as they sped away, sirens wailing.

CHAPTER FOURTEEN

Circa 1932 A. D., Pacific Northwest. Seldom had Fiana
been recognized for what she was so quickly. Poised in
a defensive stance, she watched the copper-skinned people inch
towards her with very pointy wooden staffs at the ready. She
wasn't sure how to react. Any sudden movement and she would
be dust. Literally. Typically when she met mortals, they reacted
with awe, tinged with a disquieting unease that they could not
explain and generally suppressed, only realizing her full deli-
cious horror if and when she chose to reveal herself.

These people were different.

The assembly, arrayed across the forest path in hostility,
prevented her advance or her escape. This was their place, and
they did not take kindly to strangers, especially one as strange
as she. They knew what she was, and they wanted her gone.
Destroyed even.

The one with the obvious power raised his hand, and the
mob stopped. Good. A moment to think. Perhaps this was the
power which had drawn her here in the first place. Mistake.

Think, Fiana, she thought, *This is not a time for analysis.*

She had a plan, but how could she communicate it to James?
Fiana motioned to James to move back, but he was never very
good at taking a hint. He was still too young in this life and

had not yet learned the art of telepathy. He stayed frozen next to her, his eyes transfixed on the people in the work-worn European clothes. But they were not from Europe. Far from it. These people were were spiritually connected to the powers of the earth, this land specifically, where their ancestors had dwelt for centuries.

The-one-with-power said something in a tongue Fiana didn't understand. Then he raised an object of wood, feathers, and bone, a powerful fetish, but not the wooden object she sought. She had really given up on her quest centuries ago, but every now and again misplaced sentimentality inspired her to look again. She should've learned by now what love and mercy brought her. Trouble. That's what.

He shook the totem while shouting strange words and stomping slowly towards them. The men with the pointy sticks followed suit.

James grabbed onto her arm like a scared child and squeezed.

Great. At least it wasn't her wand arm.

She felt the power in the chanted words, even though she didn't understand the meaning.

She felt its repellant violence, like a pure, tangible force driving her back.

She felt James clutching her arm tighter.

She knew she could overcome the shaman's spell eventually, but the others began leaping forward in a rhythmic dance, jabbing their spears towards her heart. With James impeding her movement and two simultaneous threats, things didn't look too good. She had to make a move or this would be the end. If she lost James in the process, it would be his own fault. Although that would be a shame. A new companion took so long to train. Sometimes, she really missed Moody.

She had to chance it now or die.

With a twist of her wrist, she released her wand from its forearm sheath, and it slipped into her hand. In a blur of movement, she both pushed James behind her and quickly parried to deflect the force of the shaman's first spell. Then, before the others could lurch forward far enough to do any damage, she fled from the wrath of mortals for the first time in centuries.

James was right on her heels. He was learning.

It wasn't a flight of panic, by the way, merely a strategic withdrawal at full speed.

They easily out-distanced their pursuers, due not only to their superior physical abilities and supernatural speed, but also their night vision which showed every detail of the forest on this nearly moonless night.

But those following were not as slow as she had hoped. Unlike the European mobs of centuries-past, they failed to stumble into obstacles or blunder into the underbrush. They also did not carry torches to destroy their own limited night vision.

The horde came on relentlessly, obviously traveling a very familiar path. Even so, she was far enough ahead of them to chance another spell. The boat was in sight. She stopped and spun around to cast another spell.

James stupidly stopped with her.

"What—" he began.

"Go! Cast off, you fool!" she cried over her shoulder.

She turned and shouted, "*Stadaim.*"

She missed. No one froze.

She certainly was rusty.

She turned and ran towards the boat as James, in his frantic state, struggled to loosen and untie the anchor rope. She pointed her wand and snapped it with a word.

Okay, not so rusty.

"See to the sail," she ordered and began to raise a wind. He did as she commanded. They were making good progress downstream by the time her pursuers burst forth from the woods. They halted on the riverbank, shaking their wooden stakes in anger. They could do nothing else now other than watch her retreat. She briefly considered a rude gesture in their general direction but didn't consider it worth the effort.

Their shaman seemed to have a plan of his own. He began a sort of ponderous stomping dance while shaking his power bundle and giving voice to a new deep, throaty chant.

She increased her wind to speed them away, but stopped when she found it increasing beyond her summoning.

That two-bit shaman was feeding her own spell! Damn that meddler.

This would soon become a grandfather storm, and they were nearing the mouth of the sea. More importantly, they were nearing dawn. Fiana desperately tried to alter the spell and move toward the land, but too much power had built up. Nature had taken over. The storm swept them out beyond the shore before they could make landfall. Now there was no choice. They would have to ride it out.

As the sun rose, she felt her power drain away, muffled as if by a heavy, wet blanket. James looked even worse than she felt. Nearly comatose, they huddled together in the tiny darkened cabin and prayed the storm's violent waves wouldn't break through the walls.

Sunlight equals dust, too.

Her kind of magic didn't travel well over water in the best conditions. And these conditions were far, far, far from best. Storm-tossed in a tiny boat was utter misery. Queasy and confused, the two vampires simply did their best to survive the long day as the wild storm drove them north and the angry waves tossed them about. Even through the dense cloud cover and plywood shelter, they felt the baleful sun sap their remaining strength. Nauseous, hungry, and weak, they continued to endure. She was not okay, but at least she didn't seem to feel as bad as James. Several times he was compelled to vomit a bloody mess into a bucket, which only made their confinement worse.

"If you don't stop fouling up our cabin, *I'll* throw you overboard!" she said, smoothing her hair back and fighting the urge to heave herself, but Fiana managed to maintain her dignity for the most part.

After hours of anguish, the sun finally began to sink. Once darkness covered them, Fiana, still far from well, felt some small strength return to her. She began working on the storm, calming it in small ways until the rains stopped and the winds relaxed to a strong breeze. She stumbled onto the deck and looked around. The sun had just dipped below the horizon, and the sky still had remnants of beautiful reds, yellows, and oranges.

James remained below, tied around a knot of despair. She started to untangle her own. Taking in her surroundings, she decided that they were not completely lost. The sight of a small island, visible and perhaps only a mile or two away, gave her some hope again. It was not impossible to reach in her weakened state, but she would have to use all her remaining strength and concentrate solely on getting to that island. They were probably in the vicinity of Puget Sound from the placement of the stars, she gathered. Some time ashore to regain her strength and maybe someone to drink, and she would be well enough to get them back to the mainland.

Looking to the tattered remains of the sail, she could see it was a lost cause. She wove the strips of cloth between her slender fingers and tried to think of an alternative. She could make James come up and row them to shore. Perhaps she could gather enough strength to propel the boat with some magic. She felt the slick shreds of former sail slide through her fingers and weighed her options. But, as it turned out, she didn't need an alternative. The boat seemed to be heading straight for the island on its own.

Very curious.

She reached out with all her senses, weak as they were. Yes. There was something out there, drawing them forward. Some new power.

My, but this was a surprising part of the world! Magic was everywhere.

Weary as she was, she let go of the sail ribbons and sat down to rest and await events. She must gather as much strength as possible from here to there. It would be best to have a few surprises ready for whatever had a grip on their boat.

Many centuries ago a small tribe dwelled on the shores of the great water. The land was bountiful, so they lived well. They showed their gratitude by adopting a local spirit as their goddess. They carved her a special talisman in the shape of a great whale in which to live. The great whale brought them many gifts, just like their goddess. They decorated the carved piece of polished wood with leather straps, strung beads, and feathers hanging from the whale's tale. They fed her with their prayers and devotion. In return, she looked after them as would a kind, but distracted mother. For generations, they prospered, but the land was too good and their numbers were too few.

New people came.

Their numbers were great and their needs even greater. With their many people came violence. The original tribe and their little goddess were pushed into an ever diminishing area. Times became hard and dangerous for them. They were facing extinction and decided to leave the shores of the mainland and find a new place where no others dwelt. They packed their possessions into their boats along with their sacred totem, which housed their goddess, and went to a distant island to live.

At first they lived well, but as the generations passed, their small numbers began to dwindle even smaller. The initially abundant resources on the island became scarce. Being so far from the mainland, they had to make do with what was available on the island. The tiny island wasn't meant to support people, so the food disappeared and the animosity among the few remaining flourished. The tribe fractured into family groups, competing against one another for survival. Without new blood to invigorate their gene pool, the people gradually died off. One day, no one from the tribe was left, save a very small goddess, alone and lonely, calling across the waters for new companions. For new believers.

Few came over the years, for those that did never returned to their homes, finding such a good and plentiful goddess on the island. But that caused the island to develop an evil reputation over on the mainland. The fishermen who plied their trade on that coast shunned the area.

So the small goddess thought on the past and began to fade away. With her small voice, she still called out across the waters for whomever would come.

Then two did come.

There was something wrong with the two figures who stumbled from the storm-wrecked boat she had drawn to her isle. These were apart, separated from unity with life. They were truly alone. Even more so than she was.

This was bad.

She could see how to reconnect them to the living world. Simply piercing their hearts with living matter would do it. But they were very, very old. Their disconnection with the circle of life was all that prevented their long overdue demise. She floundered in confusion. These creatures could not be her children.

"No," said Fiana, hearing the goddess in the wind, "but you can be my servant...Ariel."

Ariel, shocked this strange woman with the fiery hair not only knew her name but spoke it aloud, tried to hide back in the old talisman, but Fiana was too quick.

"You cannot begin to comprehend the magics I command."

There was a struggle of wills. Fiana was weak but determined and vicious. Ariel was still powerful, being a goddess, but since she had been without believers for so long, she, too, was weak. Plus she was caught unawares. This woman fed off her already-weakened energy, sucking the little strength she had into darkness. She had not experienced such darkness in all her existence. The darkness threatened to consume her completely. Ariel, so tired and lonely for so long, would've let it.

But the red-haired woman stopped.

"Oh no, dear Ariel, it is not time for you to slip from existence, for you will be of great benefit to me, as my slave." With that, Fiana waved her wand and threw Ariel back into her old talisman home, locking her inside the carved wooden whale.

Fiana, now feeling better having fed off the goddess, looked back to their boat, which lazily drifted back out to sea. She waved her wand and drew it back in, pulling it high onto the shingle.

James lay collapsed on the beach and would need many hours, maybe days, of rest and some blood to recover.

Fiana could use some blood, too.

Pity her new servant had none, but she would prove useful in other ways.

CHAPTER FIFTEEN

Max sat out on her back porch savoring the cool evening. She enjoyed the silence after spending all week at a noisy school. At one time in her life, she had listened to music almost constantly. Her infatuation went from Duran Duran in her early teens, Erasure in her twenties, and then into Annie Lennox, finding power in her soulful lyrics. But since she began teaching, she found the silence most healing. She would still listen to music in the car at times or when her soul cried out in its loneliness at home, but mostly silence. The sound of the birds or the wind in the trees soothed her as much as the harmonious piano of Billy Joel. That is, except for today. Now she needed the distraction. She needed something to divert her thoughts and calm her after the events of the day. So it was Beethoven.

The police had taken Fred away. He would probably only be seen again in sensationalized media stories before disappearing into the juvenile criminal justice system which would turn him from a disturbed kid into a career criminal. At least he hadn't actually hurt anyone. She had given her statement, such as it was, but had denied all knowledge of the strange man in green. It was funny, but she couldn't even remember what excuse she had given. Now when she thought of him, all she could think of were his lips. She tried not to think of him or his lips, but if she didn't the horror of the day came rushing back. She struggled between the two opposite images until her neighbor came out.

Max had a nice, small house. Modest, since she didn't need much. It was, after all, just her and Shadow for now. On the other side of the fence her neighbor began pounding away at something metal. It made a horrible racket and jarred Max out of her fluctuating thoughts. Then their dog started barking at the clanging. The poor thing was kept tied to a tree in the back corner of their yard, furthest from their house and closest to hers. He had dug a partial hole under her fence, and he would stick his nose through it as far his chain would allow. Max would stroke his nose and give him treats. Probably the only kindness he knew. His whole world consisted of a ten-foot radius from which he watched his family play, eat, and live at an unreachable distance. Talk about a lonely existence! He likely barked so much to say, "Hey! I'm here! Please see me! I'm over here! Can't you see me?" Craving a kind word or touch from the people to which he unfortunately belongs. Max had anonymously called animal control several times, but as long as the dog has water and is fed daily, they won't do anything.

The neighbor's wife came out next and started yelling at him, probably for making such a racket, then followed their children laughing and shouting. The cacophony of clanging, yelling, children, and barking was too much distraction for Max to bear, so she went inside to listen to Beethoven in the relative quiet of her home.

Her thoughts soon drifted back to Rowan.

Perhaps if things go well with Rowan...

She didn't finish her thought.

"Right," she said aloud, "Where would we live? The forest?"

There was always Ralph. He was—a nice man and rather handsome in his own way. Perhaps she had been too quick to turn him away. After all, his date proposal hadn't been all that unexpected. She would have to be totally clueless not to notice the way he looked at her. But she didn't feel that way about him, not like she felt about Rowan. If today, actually the last few months, had taught her anything, it was that life was fragile. It could be taken away at any moment. Did she really want to die alone? I mean, going out with Ralph wasn't settling, not really. This thing with Rowan was pure fantasy, she knew that. What would they possible have to talk about. Although, talking isn't exactly what she wanted to do.

"Stop that!" she chided herself aloud, then paused.

In that moment, she decided that she was tired of talking to herself. She was tired of coming home to no one but Shadow. It was time to take a chance on the nice guy for a change. Enough of this infatuation with the rebel type. Musicians, artists, dancers—and now a wizard? Talk about unattainable men!

"You're really living in a dream world," she told herself, "It's time to grow up."

She picked up the phone and dialed.

"Ralph?" she said at his inquiring hello. "It's Max."

She took a deep breath and continued.

"Does your offer for dinner still stand?" She smiled widely when she heard him drop something in the background. She could tell he was trying so hard to contain his excitement.

"How about tonight?" she asked. "Great! About eight? See you then."

She hung up feeling good. It was about time she did something for herself. Time to reconnect with the real world. Studly, supernatural wizards may make her feel all wiggly, but they were about as much use as the wavy-haired hottie on the cover of a romance novel: something to dream about. But for reality, a nice, real man would have to do.

Cullen trudged across the frozen lawn into the redwood forest. What a rotten day. The rottenest day of a rotten life. First the shooting, then Rowan, and then Trudy being rushed to the hospital. It was all too much! He was just a kid for pity's sake. He shouldn't have to deal with this kind of mess. At least he could get rid of Rowan tonight.

"I can hear you again," Rowan said.

Like I care, Cullen thought back.

"I didn't choose this existence, either, Cullen. Please do not be cross with me."

Where were you when I needed your help with Trudy?

"I was asleep. Doing magic drains my energy. Healing myself more so than anything else. I was tired."

Nevermind. We'll be done with each other tonight. I'm sure you're not any happier in there than I am about you being in there.

"It is not ideal, but I do not mind it as much as you do. I understand your anger, but it does not help our condition. This situation is not good for either of us. I am unable to do anything in here, and when I take over your body, it hurts you. I do have the power to maintain my form indefinitely, if I so choose, but I would not do that to you. I really am trying to minimize my impact on your life. I have lost much, and perhaps the best place for me is with my people in the Otherworld. I just wish you would have told me about it."

Cullen felt embarrassed. He did owe him at least that much. Rowan had saved their lives on more than one occasion. If it hadn't been for Rowan, they would probably all be dead.

No, he thought, unwilling to let go of his anger, *If it hadn't been for you, Fiana wouldn't be in our lives either.*

"For that, too, I am truly sorry."

Cullen could feel Rowan's remorse. His anger softened into empathy.

"You do not know me well, Cullen; but I am—was a man of action. In here, I can do little but "brood," as you put it. You must think little of me, for you have seen me at my worst."

No, Rowan, I think you're great! It's just, well, I don't particularly like you making moves on Ms. MacFey.

Rowan laughed heartily. "'Making moves on?' You make me laugh little one. I do not think of your Ms. MacFey in that way."

I feel what you feel, remember. I know what you felt. Cullen's anger was rising again, and this time he felt Rowan's embarrassment.

"Yes. A moment of weakness. That is all. My heart belongs to one woman, and she is no longer human. Still we are connected. Beyond love and desire. We share a mystical link woven through the very fabric of our magics. For us, there is and can be no others. Truly, the best place for me is away from this strange world. I hope I can make a new home for myself in the Otherworld, and you can have your body back again."

Rowan fell silent, and Cullen followed suit.

Cullen thought about life before Rowan. It was safer, but it was also dull and lonely. Was he being too hard on the wizard? He had lost everything, and especially after seeing how Trudy handled bad news today, Rowan had taken the news of his wife being a sadistic vampire quite well, considering.

Cullen walked amongst his glorious redwoods, letting them cast their spell of peace over him. Although it was winter, the Steller's Jays were still hopping from limb to limb until they disappeared from sight through the hanging moss. A chipmunk crossed his path, tail straight up in the air as he scurried away.

Cullen felt more relaxed already. The redwoods with their moist smells and gentle majesty always put him at ease.

He came to the large moss-covered rocks and the place where the Spanish Moss hung like fuzzy icicles from tree limbs all around them. Left turn here, through the clover. He was nearly to his special grove where he was to meet Moody. He didn't have to meet him for hours yet, but after being nearly shot and then watching Trudy almost die, this was the only place he could be. It was the only place he felt safe. His need for soul renewal required the solace of his personal sacred place.

He walked through the rolling mounds of clover toward his magical grove. The clover leaves were huge, nearly as big as Cullen's palms. Tiny white flowers periodically showed their bright faces through their green blankets. On happier days, Cullen liked to pick these flowers and suck on their stems. They tasted slightly sour, like a green-apple Jolly Rancher, but a bit more bitter than sour, with just a hint of subtle sweetness. Simpler days.

Green ferns sprouted up on either side of his path, set back deeper than the clover, in elegant fronds. The sea of green around him was only broken by the fallen redwood needles, which had browned in their death. Underneath it all, older needles decayed into nutrient rich soil, having rejoined the circle of life as food for the growing forest plants. Tiny insects bounced along the clover like the fairies of Cullen's dreams.

There was almost no sound among the redwoods, and Cullen liked that, too. Their immensity seemed to dampen what sounds there were, as if lost in the vastness of the forest. Although it sometimes was kinda comforting knowing that Rowan was always there, at least during those times it wasn't infuriating. He appreciated his silence now. He sensed that Rowan felt the same. They shared in the wonder of this living, silent world together.

A faint twitter of a Winter Wren or a Steller's Jay in the distance would periodically break the reverent silence among these magical giants. Then a deafening crack filled the silence: the sound of a breaking branch falling to its rest, perhaps tired of holding itself up after a thousand years.

This brought Cullen's thoughts back to Rowan. Perhaps he was tired after a thousand years, too. Even though he had not lived them. Rather, he had passed the ages suspended in time. Still, the time had passed. Cullen thought about how these monstrous trees were young saplings when Rowan had been born. Amazing. The world Rowan had known was gone, and a new, confusing one had taken its place.

He approached his favorite "bridge:" two redwood trees, fallen over two millennia ago, and now more part of the earth than the sky, formed a gully through which a tiny trickle of water flowed. They barely resembled the tress they once were. A third tree, at rest perhaps for only a century, spanned this cleft, choked with Poison-oak and huckleberry. He had learned how to identify Poison-oak the hard way. Young trees sprouted from the remains of its horizontal trunk. After crossing the bridge, he came to a monstrous felled tree which had died an inconceivably long time ago. The tangle of roots now reaching into the air was many times the height of Cullen. Turn right here, and his grove was just up ahead.

He reached his grove just as the sun began to set. It would be a cold night, but he would at least be out of the wind in his tree cave. And he could read, getting lost in the wonders of Middle-earth while he waited for Moody. Tonight he would be on another adventure of his own, for he would see the mythical Otherworld.

Cullen stood beneath the swaying giants in the place that changed his life. It was as familiar to him as the back of his hand, as the first line of his favorite book.

What would happen tonight? It certainly must be very dangerous to enter into the Otherworld and try to return.

"It is," Rowan said.

Cullen didn't reply, making it clear that he preferred the silence. He crawled inside his tree-cave, careful not to touch the walls, charred from a fire decades (or centuries) ago. It would turn whatever it touched black. The space inside was large enough for a man to crouch down, but it was a perfect fit for Cullen. From the outside, the opening looked like a slit up the trunk, like someone hadn't zipped it all the way back down. The faint slashes still could be made out along the exposed wood. He ran his hands thoughtfully over them as he had done many times before. Because of Rowan and Moody, he now knew that it was a form of ancient writing once used by the Druids called Ogham.

This grove was still his favorite place, even after everything that had happened. Bending down, he uncovered his greatest treasure: his last remaining book. No one knew he had buried it there for safe keeping, well, except for Moody, but he didn't count. He could keep a secret. No one else had known about the grove either, and he wished that was still the case. He didn't like sharing this special spot with all his friends. He had wanted to keep this to himself. He felt powerful here. He felt safe. He felt more alive than at any other time. Here he felt magical, even before he'd had a wizard living inside him. Hopefully, he would still feel magical here after Rowan was gone.

Rowan shifted uncomfortably inside his head.

The floor of Cullen's cave was mostly dirt mixed with redwood needles and twigs. He cleared away the tiny cones and other brush and sat down, leaning against the hard, bumpy interior trunk of the redwood. Cullen normally sat on his jacket so as not to get too dirty, for Trudy would have a fit if he came home covered in dirt, but today it was too cold, and Trudy wouldn't be home anyway.

He wondered if she was okay. If she still lived. Likely, the entire household would be too busy tonight to even notice his absence. Fine with him, although he was worried about Trudy.

There's no sense in worrying about things you have no control over, he thought.

So Cullen opened his only book and began to read. Moody wouldn't be there for hours yet, so he had time for an adventure or two in Middle-earth.

CHAPTER SIXTEEN

Max looked at the clock on the wall. 7:35. Time was crawling by. She checked the mirror again and touched up her lipstick. Why was she so nervous? It was only Ralph after all, the same sweet, clumsy guy she saw every day. She jumped at the knocking on the door. Wow. She really *was* nervous, but then she smiled. Ralph was early. He must be really anxious, too. She felt like a schoolgirl with a crush.

"Who is it," she said with a smile in her voice, knowing full-well who it was.

"Maddy and April," a small voice said from the other side of the door.

Or she thought she had known.

Max looked through the peep hole and saw the two young girls waiting there. She opened the door and asked, "What are you two doing here?"

"We wanted to wait with you until Cullen and Moody come back," Maddy said as she and April let themselves in. They removed their coats and threw them on the sofa, plopping down beside them, synchronized.

Max had so effectively put Rowan out of her mind by focusing on the possibilities with Ralph, that she had forgotten about tonight. Sadness filled her. She was just deluding herself with Ralph. Her heart belonged to Rowan. He would be gone from this world tonight, and he would take her heart with him. Perhaps it wouldn't work. Perhaps he'd still be here. Hope blossomed in her heart at this possibility of failure, and her hand went involuntarily to her chest.

"Hello?" Maddy said, jolting Max out of her daydream. "Anybody in there?"

"Sorry girls," Max said as she closed the door. "You can't wait here, though. They won't be back for another four or five hours yet, and I—um—I have a date," Max stammered with a little bit of embarrassed excitement.

"Oooooh!" the girls sang in stereo.

"Okay. Okay," Max said feeling genuinely happy again.

"Who is it?" April asked.

"None of your business," Max replied coyly.

"I bet it's Mr. Grims," said April playfully.

"It's not Mr. Grims," said Max flatly. "Anyway, Mr. Grims is married."

"Well who is it then?" Maddy asked through a sly smile.

"C'mon Ms. MacFey. We won't tell anyone. Promise!" April continued.

Even Maddy looked truly interested for a change.

"Well, if you promise you won't tell," Max said, playing their game. "It's Mr. Ferguson."

"Ew!" Maddy said, screwing up her face.

"I think he's very nice," April said. "Good for you, Ms. MacFey!"

"Yes, but you haven't seen him," Maddy said.

"Don't be rude, Maddy. He is very nice, and there are more important things than looks. Besides, he's not all that hard on the eyes, in a mature sort of way, something little girls wouldn't understand," Max said, crossing her arms playfully.

"No. I mean, he's okay looking. But he's so old!" Maddy said.

Max laughed out loud. "Yes. Well us old-fogies must stick together."

"Can we have some hot chocolate? It's cold out there," Maddy said.

"I'll get you each a quick to-go cup. He'll be here in fifteen minutes."

"Ooooooh!" the girls sang again.

Max rolled her eyes, but she was still smiling. They were so full of life. It was nice to have them around. Somehow their banter made her less nervous. She heated the water in the microwave and stirred the hot chocolate mix into two of her travel mugs. She could hear the two gossiping and giggling away in the next room. Kids were so very resilient. After everything that had happened last November and with the shooting today and what with Rowan leaving tonight, but there they were, acting as if they hadn't a care in the world.

She smiled to herself, glad that she called Ralph. Maybe if things went really well...

"It's really hot, so don't burn your tongues" she said to the girls as she returned to the living room, "and you can drink it on the way home." She emphasized the word "home."

"Oh, we don't have to go home, we told our mothers that we were spending—"

"Yes, that you were spending the night at each other's house. You're going to get caught one day!" Max warned, and then playfully added, "Besides, as a member of the PTA it is my duty to—"

"We'll cross that bridge when we come to it," Maddy interrupted, sounding a little too grown-up for a thirteen-year-old. She helped April on with her coat and then put back on her own coat. They took their travel mugs and headed for the door.

"You can return my mugs tomorrow, girls. Get home safe," Max said.

"Whatever," Maddy said, but she was smiling, too.

Max closed the door behind them and watched them go down the stairs into the darkness. 7:50. Only ten more minutes. She checked the mirror and touched up her lipstick. A sudden uneasy feeling made her turn around just as the front door slammed shut.

The same leather-clad vampire who had attacked her last November stood before her. She dropped her lipstick.

"Nice how invitations stand, no? What a pleasure to see you again," James said.

Cullen was jolted out of his nap by the sound of Moody's voice.

"Wake up, son! Wake up!"

Damp mist had arrived while he slept to help the darkness obscure the world. Cullen looked at his watch: 11:45—still fifteen minutes to go.

"When did you get here?"

"A few hours ago, but you looked so peaceful sleeping in your cave. But, now the time for opening the veil is nigh, and there are many things to prepare." Moody shivered and tightened his coat around his prodigious bulk. "Holy Mackrelandy, it's cold out here!" Moody got uncomfortably close to Cullen's nose, and looking into his eyes, he said, "Let me talk to the Green Man,"

"You can talk to him through me. I'm not giving up my body again, even for a few minutes," Cullen said. Arms crossed.

Moody didn't budge for a few more moments. He kept staring into Cullen's eyes at that awkwardly close distance, attempting to see past Cullen to the wizard buried deep within.

Cullen refused to back up first. This was his space, and he was holding his ground.

"That's fine, dear boy." Moody said after another moment and turned away. "I understand, but it is Rowan who must step through the veil. You must be in his form for your own protection. This is a dangerous feat we are attempting. We will be piercing puissant forces of nature. The crossing may prove too difficult for your form. Dare I say, even fatal."

Fear spread through Cullen's chest. "Well how am I to get back alone then?"

"Yes, that will be tricky."

Cullen didn't like the sound of this one bit. "Tricky? That will be tricky?! Didn't you think of that?"

"You will try to come back alone, yes; but you shouldn't go through the veil twice in such a short time. No, not in such a short time. Plus, crossing back into your own dimension, where you naturally belong, shouldn't be a problem. I hope."

He hopes. Cullen thought about the risk. Then he thought about the alternative. Living with a wizard trapped inside his head.

"Fine. Whatever. Let's just get this over with," Cullen said sullenly. He closed his eyes and tried to surrender his mind, although he braced his body for the coming pain. It came. Like a freight train it came and consumed him. Even his memory of it didn't compare to living through it again. The fierce pain seared through him, as his body stretched and tore, allowing the wizard to take over.

Then Rowan was there.

Cullen was once again trapped in his own mind.

"There you are, Green Man. Nice to see you again," Moody said, rubbing his hands together. "Fa-bu-lous."

"Marlin," the wizard nodded to him before protesting. "We cannot know that the boy will survive this journey. Why are we risking this?" Rowan asked as if he did not already know the answer.

Moody Marlin's face softened. Pity spread across it, wiping away the jolliness.

"This is no life for him, Rowan, nor is it a life for you. Something must be done. And the dangers may not be as great as you imagine. In sooth, you had once thought it impossible to cross into the Otherworld and return, but Fiana did it."

"Yes, but she is a very powerful witch. The rest of my people did not return," as Rowan spoke these words, his heart became heavy with loss.

Cullen felt the weight of his loss. He had learned how to concentrate and feel what the wizard felt in dominant form. Without this concentration, he just felt like he was alone in a very dark room.

"True, but Cullen is not without magic of his own. He just remains unaware. He has Fey blood in him, too. Yes. Fey blood," Moody said. "From my own brother. There is something else as well, a different power."

"Yes, I have felt this also. Something raw and untapped, but very faint."

This was news to Cullen, who was following their conversation with great interest.

"And my people? Why did they not return? They were more magical than any in this time."

"They were seduced by that world, Rowan. The land beyond the hills we know is very seductive. They did not wish to return. That's what Fiana told us. They were there for a year in our time, much longer for them in the time of the Otherworld. It's not that they couldn't come back. They didn't want to return," Moody explained.

"I envy you, old one," Rowan said. "You spent so many years with her, centuries by her side. It should have been me."

"Yes, Green Man. Fate is a cruel mistress, as they say" Moody replied, "but I also watched helpless as she became what she is today."

"If I had been there, it never would have happened. None of this would have happened without my cowardice. We should have died on that day. My wedding day. We all should have perished. It was our fate, but we defied that fate. Now we must endure this one."

They both stood silently.

From his confinement, Cullen could hear the wind blowing through the leaves and branches. He could hear a faint trickle of water in the distance. He could hear Rowan's broken heartbeat and feel Rowan's remorse.

Moody's beeping watch interrupted the quiet moment.

"It is time," Moody said, "to join our powers and open the way."

Together they built a sacred fire by collecting fallen wood surrounding the grove. What they were attempting was a complicated magic which required rituals as well as raw power, for Moody had not the power that Fiana had. Plus it was not Samhain; the veil must be forced open. They cast a circle and called on the four directions for assistance. Only when the sacred space was created did they begin to summon the gateway.

"*Nochd*," Rowan said.

Nothing.

"*Nochd*..." Nervously. "*Nochd*!"

Slowly, imperceptibly at first, the ever-hanging mist thickened within the grove. It coalesced into a rough oval, like a mirror hung on the air. Moody and Rowan concentrated as the center of the smoky window became clear, yet not clear. Visions of a new landscape at odds with the surrounding forest appeared, a sunlit world beyond the mist. Rolling hills hung in midair.

"Go now" Moody said, "and take this." He handed a silver rope to Rowan. "Tie this around the boy's waist when you're on the other side. I will pull him back through when you give me the signal."

"I hope this works, Marlin. It will be very dangerous for the boy,"

Cullen, hiding inside Rowan, was terrified, and Rowan was showing signs of uncertainty himself. For him, this would be a death of sorts. He would never see Fiana again, perhaps only through the mist on Samhain.

"Go through now—NOW! Before it's too late!" Moody urged.

Rowan took one end of the silver rope. Stumbling, unsure, scared—he moved forward, arms outstretched toward the window. He did not know what to expect. As his hands reached the smoke, they disappeared into it, not through it. It felt as if his hand was going through sluggish, heavy air. He pulled his hand back, overcome by fear and uncertainty.

"You must go now Rowan, please. We'll have to wait until the next Sabbat if you don't move now! Remember Fiana."

Rowan remembered. How could he forget.

Cullen remembered, too. Even though it happened fourteen centuries before his birth, Rowan's emotional vulnerability allowed Cullen access to these private memories. Memories that Rowan had shielded from him in the past. Fiana had hesitated too long, forever altering their lives. Her hesitation and Rowan's cowardice had put them in this position all those centuries ago.

Rowan deeply understood the price of procrastination, even waiting a moment too long could change everything. He strengthened his resolve and breathed in courage from the power of the surrounding trees. Closing his eyes tight, he dove through the smoky veil.

Cullen landed not on the rough, prickly ground of the forest, but on soft grass. It reminded him of the grass from his home in Ohio. Soft. Green. It smelled like it, too. Fresh cut grass. He hadn't realized how much he had missed that smell. It reminded him of home. Of family. A warm sun drove the misty chill from his body, for here it was summer. But a cool summer, almost like spring. The quiet peace of this spring morning replaced the reverent silence of the forest at night. He sat up slowly, shaking off the fall.

"Cullen" the familiar voice from his head spoke.

"Great. It didn't work," Cullen said.

"Turn around."

"What?" Cullen said, turning. There stood Rowan, just like in his dream, but real. *If any of this is real,* he thought. "Am I dreaming?" he said, pinching himself. "Ouch!"

"You're not dreaming, not now. We're in the Otherworld."

"Am I dead?"

"No, you are quite alive. We both are. Only a very powerful wizard or witch can move to the world of the dead and survive."

Cullen felt a warm satisfaction blossom within him. He was a wizard on his own after all! And this was a magical place! It was warm and sunny, but not hot. It was perfect. He looked around at the rolling green hills. Hundreds of dragonflies zipped to and fro in the air, playing in the morning sunshine. Cullen looked at them closer. They weren't dragonflies at all! They were fairies! Beautiful and graceful. Cullen wanted to run an catch them, but he remembered from an old dream that they can be temperamental. On the horizon up ahead, past the fairies, he could see the thatched roofs of a village. Before he could marvel at the tiny village too much, a huffing sound drew his attention off to his right. It was a forest! A group of unicorns had gathered at the edge to see what was going on. He was about to ask Rowan if the unicorns were friendly when he heard a faint wooshing sound behind him, far in the distance. He spun around and saw a dragon gliding through the air over stony mountains. He looked about as big as Cullen's hand from this distance, so he must've been huge!

He turned to Rowan to tell him he didn't want to go back. He wanted to stay in this magical land of fairies and unicorns and dragons. But seeing the sadness on Rowan's face, he remembered.

"What is that for?" Cullen asked, pointing to the rope. The other end of it disappeared through the veil, which looked more like a two-way mirror on this side. He could faintly see Moody on the other side holding the other end of the silver rope. He was squinting, but smiling.

"This world, it can be very alluring, but you must go back," Rowan said. "Even the crossing into your own world can be very tricky if you do not know the ways of it. This is to ensure you get back safely and not get trapped here with me, or somewhere in between."

Cullen suddenly felt ashamed. Had he been too hasty? He loved Rowan after all, in a way. It wasn't Rowan's fault, and now he was supposed to abandon him here alone. He waited for Rowan's response, but there was none.

He can no longer hear my thoughts, Cullen thought freely. He had rather gotten used to having someone around, and now he felt very alone. Perhaps he had been too rash.

"Are you ready to return, Cullen?" Rowan asked.

Cullen did not feel ready at all, but he nodded anyway.

"I'm sorry, Rowan. You've been nothing but good and helpful to me and my friends, and I've been so mean to you lately. I know it's not your fault that my life is such a mess. It's just life playing its dirty tricks on all of us. I'm sorry for wanting to get rid of you," Cullen said as a tear slipped down his cheek.

Rowan stooped down to meet Cullen at his eye level and wiped away the tear.

"It is all right, Cullen. I do not blame you for your impatience. It was a difficult situation. Now I can stay here with my people, where I belong. You can go home and be with your people where you belong. You will forget about me soon enough."

"Never! I'll never forget you!" Cullen said, throwing his arms around Rowan's neck.

Laughing gently, Rowan said, "Of course not, and you can see me every Samhain right here." He pulled Cullen away from him and looked seriously into Cullen's eyes. "The veil will open in your grove every Samhain, and we can talk through the veil briefly before it closes for another year. So we will see each other again."

This comforted Cullen a little. Rowan tied the silver rope around Cullen's waist.

"It is time to go back now," Rowan said. "Thank you for releasing me from my wand. I have learned my lesson well. I will not try to avoid my fate any longer. My fate lies here, beyond the veil. In the Summer Country."

Cullen noticed the sadness in Rowan's eyes, although he was keeping a brave face. This made Cullen sad, too. He would miss Rowan, after all. He would go back to being ordinary. *Grass is always greener,* he thought, remembering how desperate he was to get rid of Rowan just a few minutes ago.

Rowan stood up and placed his hand on Cullen's shoulder, squeezing it affectionately. Cullen rushed forward, throwing his arms around Rowan's waist and burying his head into Rowan's chest.

"I'm sorry, Rowan. I'm so sorry," Cullen cried.

"It is all right, Cullen. Be strong. You will live a normal life. It is what you deserve," Rowan said. He pushed Cullen away from him with both hands on his shoulders and looked him deep in the eyes again. "I shall be safe here, and you will have Moody to look after you on the other side. Fiana should not bother you again."

Rowan nodded to Moody, and Cullen felt a tug on his waist. The rope, guiding his footsteps pulled him away from Rowan, away from the fairies and unicorns and dragons, toward the open veil. As he passed through, he felt a cold shiver pierce his body. Rowan's image faltered and distorted. He looked as though he was in pain! Suddenly the pain was his, permeating his body with agony.

Then Cullen fell down hard on his backside on the forest floor. Moody was standing over him, and the veil was beginning to fade. He looked towards the veil to wave to Rowan as the pain receded, but Rowan was not there.

"Where is he?" Cullen cried to Moody, "Where did he go?"

"I am here," Rowan said.

Cullen spun around with unexpected joy, but there was no one behind him.

"It didn't work," Moody said.

"I am here, Cullen, back inside you. I am so sorry."

Cullen felt the familiar rage flare up and then subside. He wasn't sure if he was happy or sad. He didn't want Rowan inside him, but he was glad that Rowan was still in this world.

It's okay, Cullen thought, *Having you around isn't all that bad.*

CHAPTER SEVENTEEN

Ralph forced himself to drive the speed limit. He gripped the wheel tightly to keep his hands from shaking. Sweat condensed on his upper lip. This was date anxiety. That's all it was. He refused to think about the day's earlier events and how they were almost killed. He especially didn't want to think about that brave man in green or how she rushed to his side, while he, Ralph, sat cowering behind a table. What a loser.

"Stop it. She called you, remember," he said aloud to himself, but that just brought up the date anxiety again. He took deep, controlled breaths and squeezed the steering wheel until his knuckles turned white.

"No biggie," he lied to himself, "You see her everyday. Everything will be just fine. I'll pick her up, and we'll have a nice dinner and talk. Just talk. Like we do every day. We'll just talk. Then when I take her home and walk her to her door..."

Ralph's hands trembled so much that despite his tight grip, he nearly went off the road.

"No pressure. No pressure," he said to himself. "It will all be just fine. Just relax."

He pulled a handkerchief from his breast pocket and dabbed the sweat off his lip and around his forehead. He pushed his glasses back up onto his nose and took a deep breath, making the final turn onto Max's street. He pulled up to her house, put the car in park, and took another deep breath.

"It's just dinner," he reminded himself aloud. He grabbed the bouquet of a dozen red roses from off the passenger seat and stepped out of his car. The night was quiet. He looked down to straighten his tie. When he looked back up, there was a man dressed all in black leather on Max's porch. This gave him pause. Now the leather-clad man was going inside. He acted as if he belonged here. Comfortable and confident in his movements. Right into her house.

Ralph felt sure that she said tonight. She wouldn't have made another date. What was this man doing here?

Ralph took an uncertain step towards the house, so he could see inside. He felt foolish, standing alone with a bouquet of roses. Surely she wouldn't play him for a fool.

Max screamed. He dropped the bouquet and, to his surprise, ran towards her. He had never considered himself brave, but here he was being brave. He reached the steps just as the man in black was coming out of Max's house with Max in a headlock.

"Ralph!" Max cried, reaching out for him.

"Max!" Ralph cried, grabbing at her outstretched arms, but before he could reach her, something hit him hard on the side of the head. He found himself on the ground with his glasses knocked off. By the time he looked up, Max and her abductor were gone. Everything was a little blurry. Two figures stood before him. They looked like two girls from his Pre-Algebra class, but fuzzier. Things were not going well for a first date, even for him.

Maddy was already trying to pull him to his feet. "Mr. Ferguson! He took her. He took Ms. MacFey!" Maddy cried. April stood beside her, silently weeping. "I can't believe this is happening again, and all on the night Rowan was sent back to the Otherworld. What are we going to do without him?"

"What?" Ralph said, still a little dazed from the strike and fumbling around for his glasses. Maddy continued to try to haul him to his feet, despite his being twice her weight.

"Ms. MacFey! She's gone! He. Took. Her," Maddy said slowly, as if she was talking to a child. He felt as helpless as a child and even more confused than his first-year math students. Especially since two first-year math students stood before him and seemed to know what was going on better than he did. He did grasp that Max had been abducted by the man in black, but he did not know what that had to do with these kids or what they meant by "again" or who Rowan was or anything else really. He stuck with what he knew.

He found his glasses and got to his feet.

Okay. That's done. Now for the rest. One thing at a time.

"Took her? Where?"

"How should I know!" Maddy said. "We have to get to Moody and Rowan. Perhaps they haven't sent him away yet. No! It's only eight, they're not supposed to open the veil until midnight! We have to find them."

"Whoa. Slow down, Madeline," Ralph said. "Who are Moody and Rowan?"

"Moody is Ms. MacFey's uncle and Rowan is a wizard that lives inside Cullen. You know, Cullen Knight. He's in your class with us," Maddy said matter-of-factly.

Ralph sighed with exasperation. "Now that's just nonsense. This is no time for games, girls. If you know something then tell me. We have to call the police."

"You saw him earlier today! He's who saved us from that idiot, Fred," Maddy said in an annoyed huff, crossing her arms.

The man in green? Ralph thought.

"It's true, Mr. Ferguson," April offered, "and the police can't help. A vampire took her. She's in great danger! We have to find Rowan. He's the only one who can help. He and Moody can use their magic."

Now he was really irritated on top of being worried. "Okay. I've had enough. I'm calling the police." Ralph pulled out his cell phone and started to dial. "You girls have to learn that there is a time for fun and games, but this isn't one of them. This is very serious." But when he looked up, they were running toward the redwood forest.

It was just after midnight when the police finally left. They questioned him for hours but did nothing else useful. Twice in one day. This was becoming a habit. They treated him as a suspect, as if he'd call in his own crime. But ultimately they were satisfied he was telling the truth and left to fill out their paperwork. They said a person could not be considered missing until twenty-four hours had passed, but as this was probably an abduction, they would put out an APB just in case. They said it was probably an estranged boyfriend and that she'd be just fine. They said they didn't like getting involved in domestic disputes.

They said a lot.

They did very little.

Ralph picked up what remained of the rose bouquet after it had been trampled by a dozen cops and threw it into the passenger side of his car. Just as he was going over to his side, Madeline and April returned.

"Shouldn't you girls be in bed?" he asked, weary from the stress of the night. It was after midnight.

"We couldn't find the grove, Mr. Ferguson, and now it's probably too late!" Maddy said.

"I tried to use my magical sight, like Moody said," April offered, "but I couldn't make it work."

"Cullen took us there once, but we were too busy talking. That's a big forest! And really, really dark at night," Maddy added.

"Rowan will be gone by now and Ms. MacFey will really be in danger, especially if he takes her to Fiana," April cried.

"And Fiana is?" Ralph asked.

"Rowan's wife. She's a vampire, too"

"Of course she is. Goodnight girls, I'll see you in class tomorrow."

Ralph got into his car and drove away.

What a horrible night.

CHAPTER EIGHTEEN

Cullen had a lot to think about as he made his way back towards the Samuels' house. It seemed that Rowan would be with him forever, and there wasn't anything he or anyone else could do about it. Not unless Fiana caught him. Then he, Cullen, would be dead. Rowan would be free and also a vampire.

Moody had promised to try to come up with a new approach before he went off to his hotel, but Cullen held out little hope. He figured that he would just have to come to terms with Rowan, as he had come to terms with losing his family and having to live with the Samuels. Some things in life you just didn't have a choice. You just had to deal.

Still, it was a beautiful night. The air was crisp and still. The stars were out in their glittering profusions. There were no electric lights out there to dim their radiance or detract from their beauty. But there was a worrying glow emanating from where the Samuels' house was.

The lights were on there, which meant someone was still up. It was awfully late for anyone to still be awake. He remembered Trudy's trip to the hospital and hoped she was okay. That seemed like days ago now, but it had only been a few hours. Caught up in his own events, he had completely forgotten that the Samuels' world was falling apart. He had no idea what he would find when he got there. If it wasn't such a cold night, he would probably not go home at all, just sneak in to make breakfast in the morning and hope no one had noticed his absence.

They usually didn't.

Rex was sure to tell, of course, but one could always dream.

It was well after midnight now. After the past horrible twelve hours, first with the school shooting, then dealing with Trudy, and finally the disappointment in the forest, he didn't want to be yelled at, but he knew there was no getting around it. Again. Some things in life, you just didn't have a choice. He opened the door, ready for the onslaught of verbal abuse that was sure to follow.

But there was none.

Frank sat alone at the table, staring off into the middle distance. He held a half-full beer in one hand. His eyes were rimmed red. He looked like a zombie as he glanced over at Cullen standing by the doorway. He looked awful.

"Where have you been?" he asked sullenly.

"Studying with Maddy and April—we fell asleep," he lied.

"Okay."

That was it? That can't be it! But this must mean—did Trudy die?

"H-how's Mrs. Samuels?" he asked tentatively.

Cullen swore Frank's lower lip began to tremble a bit. He visibly squeezed his beer bottle and took an angry swig. He wiped the beer off his lips before responding.

"The doctor said she'll be fine."

"Oh. Good," Cullen said. If she was fine, why was he acting like this? Cullen decided that it was all too much to try to understand tonight. He was too tired, and he wasn't sure he even cared what Frank was feeling. He moved across the living room and turned down the hall towards his bedroom. He could already hear Rex snoring.

"Thanks," Frank said through clenched teeth, like it was painful for him to say it.

Cullen turned around, shocked.

Frank grimaced.

Cullen supposed it was him trying to smile.

"If you hadn't been here, I don't know what would've happened. So, thanks," Frank said again.

"Um. Sure. I'm glad she's going to be okay." Cullen's voice was subdued even though he wanted to yell at Frank for doing this to her, for being such a horrible bully all the time; but he knew better. Or perhaps it was just too late. After all, he had his own troubles. He still had a wizard living inside him. Maybe it was time to let Rowan take over, so he could blast the whole lot of them into next year.

Rex was already gone when Cullen awoke the next morning. The bat signal clock was projecting 9:17 onto the ceiling. He couldn't believe they let him sleep! He's late for school! That is if there even was school today. Would life just continue after the events of yesterday? He decided the entire world should just take a day off today. Fine with him. He certainly wouldn't mind just staying in bed and letting the world deal with its own problems for a while. He pulled the covers up over his head and closed his eyes. Not five minutes later, just as he was drifting back into sleep, he dimly heard a knock on the front door. Dragging himself out of bed, he went into the living room and peeked through the window. Moody, Maddy, and April stood there on his porch.

He opened the door, but didn't step aside to let them in. He hadn't let go of the hope of returning to sleep. He was in no mood for company.

"I guess you heard it didn't work," Cullen said to Maddy & April, "but I'm really worn out and the Samuels are gone, so I'm going back to bed. Can we talk about all this later."

It was then he noticed a tear fall from behind April's dark glasses. He looked at Maddy and Moody, and they both looked as though someone had died, too.

"What's wrong," he asked exhausted. Obviously there was some new problem. Great. He really didn't want to know; he just wanted to go back to sleep. A dreamless Rowan-free sleep.

"It's Ms. MacFey," Maddy said, "she's been kidnapped."

That woke him up.

"What!" he managed, his brain kicking into gear. "When? Who?"

"Kidnapped," Moody offered.

"Last night," Maddy said, "while you were in the forest."

"A vampire probably sent by Fiana," supplied April. "We tried to find you before you and Rowan split, but we couldn't. We looked for hours and hours!" Her voice trembled with trying to hold back the tears. Cullen wanted to reach out to her and comfort her, but he wasn't sure how to comfort himself.

"Fiana did this," Rowan said inside Cullen's head. It wasn't a question.

"Fiana?" Cullen asked aloud.

"Yes," Moody said. "The girls said it was a vampire, dressed all in black leather."

"The same one from before? The one that bit her last year?" Cullen asked.

"He looked exactly as you described him," Maddy said. "Tall, black hair tied back with a single black ribbon, dressed in black leather. She looked so scared, and we couldn't do anything. I mean, what could we have done?"

"It's not your fault, my dear. No, it's not your fault," Moody said, patting her shoulder. "There isn't anything you could've done."

"But I could've," Cullen said. "We could've. If I hadn't been so selfish about Rowan and—well, she would still be here. She would be safe."

"I am sure if we looked hard enough, we could find guilt enough for us all," declared Rowan. "But now is not the time for recriminations. Enough talking. Talking will not save her," Rowan said. "We must act quickly before Fiana does something horrible to her."

"You're right," Cullen said, but then remembered that the others couldn't hear Rowan. Their puzzled looks reminded him. "Rowan said we must save her. Where did they take her?"

"We don't know, Cullen," April said. "I've tried to use my, you know, magical sight, but I get nothing. I really haven't been able to see anything for months now. Maybe if I were stronger, more focused, I could be more help."

"Tell me exactly what happened," Rowan said.

"Rowan wants to know what happened," Cullen passed on, reduced to a translator.

"Well, we were spying on Ms. MacFey because she had a date with Mr. Ferguson. I mean, really? Mr. Ferguson! So anyway, we hid in the bushes and watched. Y'know, for fun. We saw Mr. Ferguson pull up in his car, but by the time he got out, that vampire was swooping into her house. It was like a blur. We didn't see him coming until he was there! Ms. MacFey screamed and then the vampire dragged her out. She was so scared. Mr. Ferguson tried to stop him, but he was struck down before he could do anything. We didn't see where he took her. Again. Blur. They were gone in a blink."

"Is Mr. Ferguson okay?"

"Yeah. He's fine. I guess he spent hours talking to the police. We tried to tell him what was happening, but he didn't believe us. We even told him what you were doing in the forest and everything," Maddy said.

Cullen chuckled at this. "Well no wonder. Would you believe a story like that?"

Maddy smiled, "Of course, but I'm wiser than most."

"Who is this Mr. Ferguson?" Rowan asked.

"He's our math teacher at school," Cullen answered out loud. His head hurt. He pinched the spaces above his eyes hard with his thumb and forefinger, pressing the pressure points and willing his head to stop hurting.

"Math was a powerful wizard, legendary even in my own time," said Rowan.

"Huh?" said Cullen.

"Math was a Druid, like me, only much more powerful than I ever was. Some say he was one of the gods even. He once made a living woman out of flowers, although that didn't turn out so well. We must enlist the help of this Mr. Ferguson, especially if he studies the magics of Math."

Math isn't a person, corrected Cullen, thinking to Rowan. *It's just short for Mathematics, you know numbers and geometry and such.*

"Then he must be wise indeed. We must go to this Mr. Ferguson and talk to him," Rowan said.

Why? Cullen thought. *He doesn't believe us. Anyway, what can he really do?*

Rowan picked up on his thought. "I would like to hear exactly what happened from another perspective. We do not know where he took her, and we need more information if we are going to help her. Perhaps this Mr. Ferguson saw something that the girls did not. It is worth looking into. How else can we find your Ms. MacFey? Even if I am in control of our body, I cannot feel Fiana strongly enough to even get a rough direction. She is too far away. She can be anywhere. She might even be close but protected by a barrier."

What kind of barrier?

"Something that would negate my magics. Earth is the element I favor, so any significant amount of moving waters would disrupt my energy flows."

"Wake up, Cullen!" ordered Maddy, giving him a light shove.

Cullen realized that they had all just been staring at him during his conversation with Rowan. He must've just looked lost in thought.

"Hey, I was talking to Rowan," he protested.

"So, what does he have to say?"

"He wants to talk to Mr. Ferguson. See if he saw something you didn't."

"I told you what happened!" Maddy said defensively, "besides, Mr. Ferguson doesn't believe any of this stuff anyway."

"I told him that."

"The Green Man is right," Moody said, "We must talk with this Mr. Ferguson. Yes, indeed. Find out what he knows. What he saw. Perhaps even how he can help. Ne c'est pas?"

The much-discussed Mr. Ferguson sat alone in his basement, surrounded by gadgets and strange machines. Against one wall, a large dry erase board squirmed with formulas and scribblings, indecipherable to any but Ralph and perhaps a dozen other specialists in the world. Elsewhere in the room were three computer stations: two showing constantly revolving screen savers and one that was just a paperweight. He kept it for spare parts. Book shelves and book piles were scattered liberally around. In between was a work bench covered in circuits, diodes, chips, and molded plastic. Below this were shelves of completed, but esoteric, gadgets. Above, a glass case displayed a nerdvanic collection of original Star Wars action figures. Still in their original boxes.

He stared at the wall in a comatose daze. His eyes were red rimmed and bloodshot. The kind of red that followed a night of partying or crying.

He hadn't been partying.

He had been awake all night thinking. Working. Worrying. Trying to figure out a way to find her. To save her. Even though he might wish it, he knew he wasn't the swashbuckling kind who could swing in on a chandelier and save the girl with some fancy swordplay. He would need to find another way. Before that, he would need to know where she was. And even before that, he would need to know what was really going on.

He picked up a perfect replica of Luke's light saber, regarding it for a moment. Feeling the weight of it in his hands.

Then the questions returned.

Who was that strange man in black leather? What was he doing to her? Does she know him? Is he a former boyfriend? Is he hurting her? Violating her?

Dropping the light saber on his desk, Ralph grabbed his head, his fingers splitting his hair into messy tangles at the thought of it. He tried to put the worst out of his mind. He had to focus on ways to save her rather than worry about what might or might not be happening. Imagining what she was going through would do no one any good.

He couldn't figure it out. If only he had taken a sampling of her energy signature for his research. Maybe, just maybe he could trace it; but that, too, was a long shot even with the correct data. And he didn't have the correct data, *so think of something else Ralph. Think!*

There was too much emotional turmoil for cognitive focus.

"Huh, some genius," he said to no one. A tear slipped down his cheek. He angrily wiped it away. "You're an idiot, Ralph, not a genius. How could you have let this happen? If you had been there just a few minutes earlier. Why did I wait so long to leave? Trying to be cool about it all, you fool. You'll never be cool. You're just a nerd, and you'll always be just a nerd. God! I'm such a loser." Ralph sank lower into his own self pity. He picked up a strange instrument and hurled it at the dry erase board. It clanged as it hit and scratched the ink off part of one formula in thin streaks. He picked the light saber back up, and reared back to hurl it across the room as well. But then he thought better of it and instead laid it down gently on its display stand.

He took his glasses off and threw them down. With his elbows resting on the table, he buried his face in his hands and wept silently.

There came a faint knocking sound from above. Ralph sat up straight, wiping away his quiet tears with the palms of his hands as he did so. The knocking came again, more loudly.

Ralph pulled a handkerchief from his pocket and wiped his face down. He picked up his glasses and cleaned them as he began to climb the stairs to the door.

It's the police, he thought. *I know what they've come to tell me. Oh god! This can't be happening. This can't be happening. If only I had asked her out sooner. If only I wasn't such a coward.*

His thoughts became ever more self-deprecating until he reached the door. He put his glasses on, took a deep breath, and bravely opened the door.

It was Madeline, April, Cullen, and the strange roundish man from the cafeteria. He blinked at them stupidly, unable to comprehend their presence on his doorstep.

"I'm sorry, I'm not in the mood for visitors," he began.

"Tough cookies," Maddy said, "We have to talk to you." She pushed past him into his house.

"Yeah. It's important," April said, following Maddy, who was surveying the interior with hands on hips in search of a meeting place.

Cullen just stood there silently. The look on his face reflected exactly what Ralph felt. Shame, self-pity, regret...love.

Moody swept off his fedora and bowed. "Mr. Ferguson, sir, my name is Marlin, and I am a relative, of sorts, to Maxine. May we please come in. We have much to discuss. Things of great importance, my chap."

The antiquated courtesy of this spherical man knocked Ralph off guard. As if he didn't know what he was doing or why, he stepped aside and let the rest of them in. They all crowded in the corner of Ralph's small living room. There certainly wasn't enough room for them all to sit down, especially Moody.

"My dear man," Moody continued, "Maxine may be in great danger, and we need to act quickly. The thing that took her will be taking her to my lady. My former dark mistress, and she is in great, great danger there."

"Thing? What do you mean the thing that took her?" Ralph asked.

"He was a vampire! We told you last night," Maddy said, a little miffed.

Ralph looked to the adult of the group for some sign of explanation for the wild accusation. But Marlin looked very serious.

"You're all insane," Ralph said with a wave of his hand, backing up slowly. "Please leave." He held the door open, expecting them to oblige.

"It's true, Mr. Ferguson," a small voice said. Ralph looked down at Cullen, who stood there with his head bowed. "It was a vampire who took her, and he took her to the meanest, most dangerous vampire alive."

"Fiana," Maddy said.

"Rowan's wife," April continued.

Ralph, stunned and angry at the same time, threw up his hands, turned around, and went back down into his laboratory in the basement. "Close the door on your way out," he shouted back at them.

But they didn't leave. Instead, they all followed him down into the basement, like a single file of soldiers.

Ralph was too weary to argue. He collapsed back into his chair, ripping his glasses off and pressing the palm of his hand into his throbbing temple.

"Wow!" Maddy said, picking up a strange gadget.

"Don't touch that!" Ralph chided.

"What is all this stuff?" Maddy asked, ignoring him.

"It's my research," Ralph responded, physically taking the instrument out of her hands and putting it back where it belonged. "Waste of time, really. Nothing that can help her."

"My dear man, please tell me what you saw. I know all this sounds crazy to you, but just humor us. What did you see last night?" Moody said.

Ralph sighed heavily from exhaustion, giving in. "Fine. Just as I told the police umpteen times last night, I went to her house. As I approached the door, a man dressed all in black rushed passed me with Max in a..." his voice trailed off to avoid breaking. He composed himself and finished by saying, "I tried to help her, but he must've knocked me down because the next thing I knew I was on the ground and he was gone. She was gone."

Ralph sat down hard at his desk, throwing his glasses down and covering his eyes for a moment. Pulling himself together, he put his glasses back on and looked up, but didn't see Maddy fiddling with one of his machines until it was too late.

"What does this do," she said as she flipped the red switch. It whirred on in an instant. Cullen began screaming and clutching his chest. Beams of light shot between his fingers, and Ralph watched in disbelief as Cullen's body stretched and broke. It was as if the machine was pulling him apart.

"Turn it off! Turn it off!" Ralph shouted at Maddy, rushing over to her. He pushed Maddy out of the way to get to the controls, which caused her to knock into April, who knocked into the morphing Cullen. Visible energy bolts surrounded them both. April screamed.

Ralph shut the machine down, but the energy from it did not stop.

"April," Maddy cried, lunging for her. She tried to pull her out, but instead she got trapped with April and the transforming boy.

"I'm so sorry," Ralph stammered. He ripped the plug out of the wall, but the energy continued. He was horrified.

Even Moody stood there dumbfounded.

Cullen had never changed like this before. It was normally something he couldn't control when he was scared, but now he was fighting the change, trying to keep control of his body.

"Let go, Cullen," Moody said, "for goodness sake let go!"

April and Maddy writhed in pain along with Cullen, trapped in the magic.

"Let go!" Moody pleaded.

Suddenly, the streams of energy stopped and Rowan sat between the girls on the ground.

"Oh my god," Ralph said.

He took his glasses off and then put them back on.

"Oh my god," Ralph said again. "What's going on? How is this possible? This can't be real. Everything you've said. It can't be real."

"Where is Maxine?" Rowan said to Ralph sternly, getting up from the ground.

Ralph looked at him with his mouth hanging open.

Moody helped the girls up from the ground. "Are you girls okay?" he asked.

"I can see again," April said, "and I have a headache."

Tears streamed down Maddy's face.

"What's wrong, my dear?" Moody asked.

"The pain. All the pain!"

"Are you hurt," Ralph said, rushing over to her and forgetting about the green-clad wizard for a moment. He checked her for cuts.

"No. Your pain. His pain—" pointing to Rowan "—It's too much. It's too much. Make it stop," she said, clasping her hands over her ears as if she could stop the sensation.

"What's going on?" Ralph demanded, now more annoyed than worried.

"As we told you before, dear man," Moody began. "This is Rowan. He dwells inside Cullen, as you saw."

"But how? I mean—how?"

"We do not have time for this now," Rowan barked. "Where have they taken her. What did you see?" Rowan moved so quickly over to Ralph, that Ralph stumbled back and had to catch himself against his work table. His glasses got knocked sideways on his nose, and Rowan stood a little too close for comfort.

I just saw a boy morph into a man, he thought. *It wasn't just the trauma of the shooting. I really saw it!* Ralph stood looking dumbfounded at the wizard before him.

"What did you see!" Rowan repeated even more sternly than before, closing the short distance between them. Anger filled his eyes, and Ralph cowered.

"I—I didn't see anything," Ralph stammered, straightening his glasses. They were about the same height, but Ralph certainly felt smaller next to Rowan. "Just what I told you—um, Cullen and the others before. There was a man dressed all in black who took her. He knocked me down, and when I got back up, they were gone. I didn't see a car. I didn't see anything else!"

"I'm sure it's Fiana, Rowan," Moody said, holding both April and Maddy protectively close against his massive middle. "Cullen said it sounded like the same man that attacked her last year."

"Yes, I remember the creature well. He had a morbid power about him. I got there too late to keep Maxine from being hurt, but I did stop him from killing her then. It all but drained me to do so. He is very strong."

"He tried to kill her before?" Ralph said, finding a little confidence from somewhere and standing up tall next to Rowan. He was actually becoming angry now. It seems there had been a lot going on, and he was coming in at the climax. It was time to be decisive. Past time. "We must find her. Tell me more about this Fiana. Is she like you? The girls said she was your wife."

"And you didn't believe us," Maddy chided.

"The situation has changed, Madeline," Ralph said, "It sounded like crazy-talk. If I'd only believed you, we wouldn't be starting—" He looked at his watch. "—eight hours later! For that, I apologize. But how could I have believed such a story without empirical data? I believe you now. So let's not waste any more time. Please, just tell me everything, and I'll do my best to believe you no matter how crazy it sounds."

"It's probably too late," Maddy snapped.

"I won't believe that," Ralph said, shaking his head. If he believed it hard enough, Max would have to be okay.

"We must work as if she's still alive and unharmed until we are certain it is otherwise," Moody said.

"Please, tell me everything," Ralph insisted again.

Then great stories were told of events from ages past. Moody explained what had happened centuries ago, and how he came to be in Fiana's service. He told of the great love she had for Rowan and her single-minded quest to find him and release him from the wand. He told of her sacrifices throughout the ages, and of the ultimate sacrifice of her soul. He told how she fought the darkness for five hundred years, but the cruelty of the world finally wore down her resolve. He told of how she became evil and cruel and how Moody, himself, had fallen from her favor. He told of how Cullen found the wand and how he and Rowan came to share a body. He told of the showdown in San Francisco and how he, Moody, was released from Fiana's grasp through the help of Max, Cullen, and the girls. He told of the powers that Maddy and April had acquired in that conflict.

Ralph sat stunned. He tried his best to absorb what his mind instinctively wanted to reject. "Wow," he finally said, "it's all true. Magic. Vampires. Supernatural forces. It's straight out of Dungeons & Dragons. It's crazy. Where does this leave physics? Are all my calculations mere concoctions of Descartes's Malevolent Being?"

"Huh?" Maddy said.

"The whole proof of mathematical legitimacy relies on the existence of an omnipotent, benevolent being," Ralph continued, still talking to himself. Running his hands through his hair and laughing, he concluded, "And I'm an atheist!"

"No, no," interjected Moody. "It is not all true. That is to say what I have spoken of is true, but magic is not unscientific. Your theory of strings and the unified field are very close, with the interconnection of everything and overlapping energy fields and such."

"Energy fields, really?"

"Enough," declared Rowan, "We can not just discuss philosophy while Fiana does as she will. We must act, preempt her plans before they bear their evil fruits."

"What do you suggest, Rowan? Do you know where she is? Can you feel Fiana?" Moody asked.

"No. She must be too far away. She could be back in Caledonia on the other side of this world. Or she could be very close and surrounded by water."

"What do you mean?" Ralph asked.

"Water mutes our magic. It masks it. If she is surrounded by water, it blurs my sensitivity to her."

"We're near a coast, so she could be close," April said.

"She could be anywhere," Maddy said, rubbing her temples. This entire episode had left her with a headache as well.

"The young one is right. She can be anywhere," Rowan repeated. "But even if she was close, we have no way to find her."

Ralph became thoughtful, tapping his temple with his index finger, as he walked over to his pile of electronic gadgets. He selected one and switched it on. As he suspected, it began going ballistic, showing wild, exciting readings like he had never seen! A spark of inspiration ignited within him. He turned back to

Rowan. "Is she like you?" he asked Rowan. "I mean, I know she's a vampire, which will obviously complicate her emanations."

"Obviously," Maddy said with more than a hint of sarcasm.

Ralph was exhilirated, and he found it difficult to contain the hope flourishing in his mind. He could hardly formulate words in his eagerness. "But does she have this—" He searched for the right word. "—*power* about her? This field of energy?"

"She was a very powerful witch before she gained her vampiric powers, if that's what you mean," Moody said.

"Yes," Rowan agreed. "She was very powerful. Equal to my power in our time. We were called upon to serve the god and goddess."

"I think I can find her! I mean, it's a long shot, but I think I can find her!" He tinkered with the gadget in his hand some more before continuing. "According to these readings here." He looked back down at his gadget and fiddled with some of the buttons and knobs and settings. "See here," he said, turning the gadget so that Rowan and the others could see. "This is your energy signature. It's much, much higher, much more powerful than anyone or anything I've ever come into contact with, that wasn't radioactive. If Fiana's is similar, I might be able to zero in on it and trace it. Then we can follow the signal to where she is and save Max!"

"This machine can tell you where Fiana is?" Moody asked in amazement.

"I think it's our best shot, but I'm willing to entertain other ideas," Ralph said, now full of confidence, "Not that I think we have any." All his tinkerings and research might actually be worth something after all!

No one said anything. They all just looked at each other in silence.

"Great! It's set then. All I need to do is tap into a satellite signal and upload a sample of your energy signature. You will have to—er—change back to Cullen or you will cause it to give a false reading."

Ralph spun around and started working feverishly over his desk. He scribbled formulas down on paper, adjusted more knobs and switches, and then transferred them to the dry erase board after he wiped away what had been there with one big swoop.

The other four watched.

Finally, Moody said, "It's worth trying. His observation is also correct; we don't have another plan."

"He sure feels different. I feel hope inside him now. A lot of hope and love," Maddy added. She seemed recovered from the ordeal with Rowan.

"It's different this time," April said. She had been quiet for a long, long time, but since everything was rather chaotic, it went unnoticed.

"What is?" Moody asked. He let go of both the girls now that they had recovered.

"My sight. It's different than when we were in San Francisco."

"How?" Moody asked.

"Stronger." Maddy replied. "I feel everything more intensely than before."

"Yes. Stronger," April confirmed.

"It is because you were in direct contact with me as I changed," Rowan said.

"Yes! Last time, it came to us through that vampire guy," Maddy said. "Can I just say 'Ew'!" she added, as the memory of being covered in vampire dust followed.

"Does this mean it will last longer this time?" April asked.

"Perhaps."

"I can see colors now. I mean, I guess they're colors. They're something. Last time it was all like one color in different shades."

Ralph was working feverishly, mumbling to himself. He was entering data at one of the computer stations. He had strapped a Boba Fett helmet with added wires and sensors protruding from odd places to his head.

"Almost ready," he said, as he noticed all of them watching him. "You're going to have to turn back into Cullen. Can you do that?"

"Of course."

Then all eyes were on Rowan. Ralph especially watched closely. He didn't even blink, for he didn't want to miss a second of it. And, it only took about a second. If he had blinked, he would've missed it.

"But—" Ralph began, pointing to Cullen and looking at Moody for an explanation.

"Rowan didn't fight the change," Moody said matter-of-factly.

"Of course!" Ralph said and his face lit up with understanding. He turned back to his notes, erased frantically, and then scribbled down some more. After adjusting a knob or two on his gadget he said, "Ready to give it a shot?" There was a gleam of excitement in his eye.

As he flipped the switch on his device, the large machine behind them whirred into life and a computer screen came on behind him. It was a map of the world. In fact, it looked suspiciously like Google Earth. "I've tapped into a few useful sites and integrated their information to create what I needed rather than starting from scratch," he explained. "Some of what I did may not be technically legal since I am commandeering some satellite equipment I'm not even supposed to know about, let alone make use of, but I'm not causing any harm and no one should even notice my presence," he justified.

Circular waves blipped on the screen, covering the entire earth. Nothing else happened. Nothing changed. After nearly five minutes, the kids began shifting uncomfortably.

Ralph cleared his throat nervously. "Well, I don't think that worked," he admitted. "Let me try something else."

He tapped away at the keyboard some more and drove the mouse around its R2D2 mouse pad a while before hitting ENTER and sitting back to observe. Again, circular blips, but this time they began to concentrate along the West Coast of North America. As they got smaller, they moved farther North until they stopped off the coast of Washington. They watched fascinated for what seemed like a long time, but really took just over a minute.

"There," Ralph said with great pride. "It worked!"

"Fa-bu-lous!" Moody said.

"How do you know that's her?" Maddy asked.

"Well, I don't. I just know that it's an energy signature as strong as Rowan's and with an almost identical range, but reversed. It might be nothing, some anomaly. But there is only one way to find out, and we've already wasted too much time."

"What do you mean 'reversed'?" asked April.

Ralph answered her question as he swooshed together papers into a messy pile and stuffed it into a well-worn backpack along with more gadgets. "All of our energy fields are interconnected with the field around us, but Rowan's is much larger and stronger than usual. It is a kind of symbiotic relationship with all fields becoming stronger through their interaction. Fiana's field doesn't operate that way. She has a sort of negative field which drains the energy of everything around her."

"Of course!" Marlin said, getting drawn back into a philosophical conversation. "It makes sense being a dead thing herself, no longer of this world—"

"Can we get going now?" Cullen interrupted, "Ms. MacFey could be hurt."

He had been so quiet, they had all almost forgotten he was there.

"Or dead," Maddy said.

"She's not dead!" Cullen yelled at her.

Maddy pulled back, offended at his outburst.

"How are we going to get there? I mean, it's like a day's drive or more," April said.

"First of all, *we* are not going anywhere. I am going—and you, too, Moody. But you kids are staying here," Ralph said.

"Are you insane, man? Did you not just feel the power of Rowan yourself? We must have him there to fight Fiana. Do you think you can fight her with your gadgets?" Moody said.

"Hmmm. Good point. I was hoping we could sneak her out, but we have no idea where they have her or—"

"Fiana will smell you coming a mile away!" Moody laughed.

"She's really dangerous, Mr. Ferguson," April said.

"And you're not leaving us behind anyway!" Maddy said, glaring at him through a furrowed brow. "We can help! We helped last time!"

"Ok. Ok. There's no time to argue, but we don't have a car big enough for us all."

"We won't be taking a car," Moody said.

CHAPTER NINETEEN

M ax was tossed to the ground beside a frighteningly familiar black car. Her legs collapsed under her before she could will them to support her. What was going on? Her thoughts were obscured by a fog of indolence. Surely she should panic. Why weren't her veins overflowing with adrenaline? She was certainly terrified, so why was she not acting terrified? Why could she summon no resistance? Was she drugged?

James seemed to expect nothing from her. He let her lie where she had crumpled to the ground while he walked around and opened the vehicle's trunk.

"Get in," he ordered.

Now she could move. She climbed into the trunk. She didn't want to, but she seemed to have no control over her body. It was as if it was acting on its own. Why wasn't she running? Why wasn't she calling for help? Why was she lying down in the dark trunk?

He must be doing something to control me, she thought. *I should resist. Run away. Scream. Do something!*

She opened her mouth to scream, or at least she thought she did. She thought it. She decided to do it, but for some reason it wasn't happening. It was like when you're cuddled up on a Saturday afternoon reading a book or watching a movie. You really think you should balance your checkbook or exercise. Your mind decides that's a good idea, but your body just doesn't move. It was like that, only not at all comforting like a warm couch and a good book.

The trunk lid closed, sealing her inside.

They drove for hours. Eventually she slept.

When the car finally stopped, she was wide awake. She heard the driver's door open. She felt the car rise and bounce as the driver stepped out.

Dreadful anticipation was rife, spreading through her mind with every deliberate step she heard approaching the trunk.

The trunk opened.

It was still dark outside, or dark again, but not as dark as the trunk had been. She had no way of knowing how much time had passed, but she was ready to act this time. Her mental fog had cleared somewhat, as she had been wrestling against it ever since she woke up in the blackness of the trunk. She launched herself out of the car and began a stumbling run with cramped legs.

"Stop!" James commanded, dashing after her. She wasn't hard to catch, as she stumbled and fell, cursing her body's betrayal. James leapt upon her and dragged her back toward the car. Despair overcame her when she saw Fiana glaring at her with evil satisfaction.

"Your control seems somewhat lacking," she remarked to James coyly. "Perhaps you should bite her again."

"It would be my pleasure."

Max whipped around to look at James, teeth bared, and screamed.

Fiana laughed. "Just a little one," she said. "We do not want her damaged too much—yet."

Even before she felt the prick of his teeth, Max's scar from the old wound began to throb in unison with the new one, only a few hours old. It was just a prick at first. He was toying with her. But then it came, the piercing pain of her flesh being punctured and penetrated. The mental darkness rose within her once again.

He drank for what seemed like hours. Max stopped struggling after a moment or two and just endured. He controlled her again.

"Enough." She heard Fiana say. "Remember, we have another use for her. My dear husband will not ransom the dead. It is time to send him a message."

She was barely aware of the boat trip, as she struggled to regain self-awareness. Weak from the loss of blood, she assumed. It must be that. But there was more, and she knew it even if she wouldn't let herself admit it. There was a darkness coursing through her veins with the blood she had left, a poison of despair invading her natural sanguine demeanor. She could feel herself being drawn away from the light and into the darkness.

Thirst overcame her. She had no idea how long it had been since she'd had anything to drink. The loss of blood only added to her thirst. They were surrounded by water, but there was nothing to drink.

"Water," she managed. "Please."

"We'll get you some water and food when we reach the island," Fiana responded coldly. "You must regain your strength for James to enjoy you longer."

James wrapped his arm around her neck and pulled her lasciviously close to him. Disgust overcame the thirst. Yet, she couldn't not move. For the rest of the journey, she tried to think of anything else. Ralph. Rowan. Normal life. Sunshine. It helped a little.

She saw little of the shore when they finally docked at a small wooden pier. With sinking hopes and no will of her own, she followed Fiana and James through a large Tudor-style manse and down into an underground cell carved into a natural cavern. The small barred opening on the back wall let in the outside air, but she could see nothing through it. It was cold. She was cold, and she certainly wasn't in Fortuna anymore.

"What does this woman have with dungeons, anyways?" Max said to herself. She sat back in a corner and wrapped her arms around herself in a feeble attempt to keep out the damp cold. She pictured herself on her couch, cuddled up with her lap blanket and a hot cup of mocha. She took several deep breaths and blew them out, each time, picturing roots stretching down from her spine, going into the earth. She channeled all the fear down those roots and tried to calm herself.

Wait until sunrise, she thought, *that's when they are weak. Perhaps I can find a way out then.*

She didn't think about what to do if she could find a way out. Swim for it? She would cross that bridge when she came to it. For now she would try to focus on herself. She would do what she could to purge the filth of James from her soul. It would take a lot of effort and time. But it seemed time was all she had at the moment, although she might not have very much time. Who knew what they had planned for her. She comforted herself by rationalizing that if they wanted her dead, she'd already be dead. Of course, there were worse things than death.

Perhaps they would just keep her and feed off of her slowly for months.

Perhaps they would turn her. That was worse than death.

She pushed such thoughts from her mind each time they crept back in. She focused on channeling the darkness down into the earth and drawing healing light from the universe.

She heard a scuffling somewhere nearby, but she couldn't see a thing. It was blacker than black. That scuffling could be rats, or worse, cockroaches! She shuttered at the thought and tried to push it from her mind. But images of cockroaches crawling all over her body crept back in.

She stood up, brushing herself off just in case, hoping that moving her body would quiet her mind. She felt along the wall to where she saw the small barred window. Perhaps she could see a star or some kind of distant light. Anything. Please, just any sort of light. Wrapping her hands around the bars, she put her face near the opening. Nothing. Just blackness. She couldn't see where the water ended and the sky began. There was no horizon, only darkness. Her thoughts returned to death. She wondered if death was like this. Just nothingness. No light. No hope. No love. But also no despair or hate. Falling into the blackness of the no-horizon night, she felt she began to understand death. It didn't seem that bad.

Hours later, she was still in the dark, but it had lessened, both inside herself and outside her cell.

CHAPTER TWENTY

This really was a rare treat for Trudy. It wasn't often that she could convince herself to spend forty dollars on something she could do herself. But that wasn't really the point, was it. Plus, it just wasn't the same when she did it herself. It really took some skill and a steady hand. The point was the luxury of someone else doing something for you. It was about pampering oneself. It was about treating oneself with care and respect. Then, of course, there was the gossip. The "Get Nailed & More Nail Salon" was a regular clearing house of information. Better than any newspaper, with in-depth analysis imparted with such obvious pleasure. As Trudy walked into the converted living room to the sound of a spring-suspended bell, her old friend Stacy looked up from her gossip rag and gave her a sympathetic smile. It took but a moment for Trudy to feel relaxed as she inhaled that unique nail salon smell with an ecstatic sigh. It was like the smell of fresh baked cookies to a child: pure heaven. Here is where she belonged—being pampered! Where people waited on her, quite literally, hand and foot.

Stacy led Trudy to a soft brown pedicure chair, turned on the massage feature, and then placed her fingers in a glass bowl full of solution. It reminded Trudy of those old Palmolive commercials where Madge the Manicurist would soak her clients' hands in Palmolive dishwashing liquid. Within the comfort of the spa pedicure chair and the commiserating chatter of Stacy, Trudy began to feel safe again.

"Oh my dear, Trudy," Stacy said as she filled up the small tub at the foot of the chair. She removed Trudy's shoes and placed her feet in the warm water before returning to her unsoaking hand, inspecting it to see what would be needed. "I've been hearing the wildest rumors!"

"Well, if it's that I'm married to a lying cheat who fathered a bastard with my neighbor, then the rumors are true."

Stacy gasped in dramatic outrage.

"What? That stupid swine! He has no idea how lucky he is to have a woman like you. And to have you put up with him for so long!"

"Don't I know it! But his luck has ended. I'm through with being tied down to that loser. If he wants that woman so badly, than he can go live with her. Because I tell you this: he's not going to be living in my house anymore. Let's see how she likes feeding and cleaning up after his fat ass. I've had enough."

"You go girl." Stacy said with an around the world and back air snap. "You don't need him. There are plenty of good men out there who would be grateful for a lady like you. I say good riddance."

That's right. Trudy thought. *I am a lady, and I do deserve more.*

"Men! Ha!" Trudy said. "Who needs men anyway? I can manage just fine on my own, especially with the alimony. I mean I've already got a child. I certainly don't need an overgrown, self-centered second child anymore. Can you believe he's been secretly giving her money all these years? No wonder we never have enough!

"Don't you have two?"

"Two?"

"Two kids."

"Oh yeah. That one. And who's bright idea was he?"

"Isn't he your nephew?"

"Not really. Some kind of really distant fourth cousin-twice removed-by marriage, thing. Not really a relation at all."

"Why did you take him in then? Don't they have agencies for that?"

"Oh, that was what's-his-face's idea. There was supposed to be some trust or something that he wanted to get his hands on, plus he said there would be a check from social services every month for the boy's upkeep, so we took him in. Frank's always been in a dead-end job and has never made enough money, and he's always looking for an easy way out. He's even tried MLMs once or twice. What an idiot! Always looking for the easy way out. Plus, things were tight."

Trudy paused to catch her breath and remembered how much she stressed about spending this forty dollars on herself today. "What do I mean were? Things *are* tight. They're always tight."

Stacy continued filing Trudy's nails, listening attentively.

Trudy swished her feet around in the warm water of the foot bath and scowled, thinking about all the things she had given up and done without because of her lazy loser of a husband. "Of course it was an easy answer for him," she continued, "he didn't have to care for the boy. I did. I do it all. I always do it all. But then we learned that this trust is untouchable until he graduates from high school. So that's out until he's seventeen. If he wasn't a year ahead, we would never see it at all because it would go directly to him. It better be as much as Frank says it will be. The support check doesn't cover much, so the only reason we're holding on is the hopes of a six-figure trust, at least. Frank says the boy is from old wealth. Still, they won't tell us, and I'm really tired of waiting."

Trudy felt a twinge of something resembling guilt. It was Cullen who had called the ambulance after all. If it hadn't been for him, then she likely would've died. Nevermind that! One good deed doesn't erase six years of ingratitude, she decided.

Stacy carefully set down Trudy's left hand and lifted the right out of the solution, inspecting it critically before working on it.

Trudy took a few deep breaths and began to relax again. She was getting herself too worked up, and this was supposed to be a tranquil experience. The hospital visit and the events that put her there had been very traumatic. She had nearly died, or that's what they told her. Frank was very apologetic and started begging for her forgiveness.

Too little, too late, sweetheart.

"You know, they denied Fred bail pending psychiatric evaluation?" Stacy said, breaking the momentary silence.

"You mean the bastard-child? I never did like that kid. I guess I should've suspected something when they moved from Texas just about the same time we did. God! I'm so trusting!"

"You are a saint, Trudy," Stacy said. "You deserve so much more."

"That kid needs to be committed," Trudy continued. Her face was screwed up in a most ferocious scowl. "He's the crazy spawn of that insane home-wrecker and a seriously deficient father. He can come to no good. I'm just glad my own boy takes after me! He is such an angel and to have been fathered by such a..."

A few hours and much gossip later, Trudy walked out with her french manicure and pedicure, long enough to be considered claws in both places, and a determination to get on with her life without a loser husband holding her back.

As she admired her french manicure, she decided she'd start with a trip to Paris, right after the divorce settlement. After all, she'd be getting alimony and she'd no longer have to feed his gluttony. She'd save so much that she could spend a whole week in the elegance of Paris.

It was decided. She just had to figure out what to do with Cullen. Maybe a cheap boarding school if there was enough money. Military for preference.

Since Moody needed four or five hours to make arrangements, they decided to disperse until late afternoon when they would meet up again at Ralph's house. Ralph himself would spend the time adapting and preparing some of his instruments and inventions. Moody's insights on magic had provided Ralph with a breakthrough on his energy field research, so there was much to do.

That's why he had shooed them away. The kids were happy to have just stayed there to wait. Where else would they go? The girls had gone off to make requisite visits to their homes and beg for another night of sleep overs. They used yesterday's shooting as an excuse of not wanting to sleep alone.

Cullen, who had no intention of dealing with the Samuels on what might be his final day on this earth sought solace and rest in his special grove. His adventures of the previous night and the wearing worries of the day soon tossed him into sleep. Cullen dreamt, and as had happened before, he dreamt of Rowan. They were in what Cullen now accepted as *their* grove, the place where he had found the wand. The sun was somewhere beyond the trees, but inside it was cool and shady. The dream wasn't a pleasant one. They had been arguing about magic for awhile, and Cullen had grown irritated and surly.

"Why don't you just do away with Fiana with like a spell or something," Cullen asked, "Or cure her from vampirism or at least make her sane."

"Cullen, listen to me," Rowan entreated. "This is important."

"Important how," snapped Cullen. "Important like your precious wife who's running about killing people? Or just a little important like the ruin you two are making of my life?"

"This is world important, beyond you. Beyond me. Beyond even Fiana. I'm talking about the fundamental underlayment of reality."

"Which you seem to be able to bend to your will," cut in Cullen.

"It's not as simple as that. There is an equilibrium which must be maintained. When I exert my will upon something, I can change its nature, but only so far as there is a path for that change to follow. The narrower that path, the harder it is to affect the change."

"It seems to me you just point your wand and say the magic words and poof! The bullies are mice."

"Have you ever studied rodents? Their whole lives are hunger and fear. Running. Hiding. Consuming whatever they can. But when faced with danger, they bristle and act vicious to intimidate whatever threat they perceive. Rex and his friends were the same way. They act tough to hide the fear which rules their lives. Changing them into mice took very little effort, since it was merely an adjustment of their outer forms. Someone with a greater sense of self and will like Fiana would not be affected so easily.

"As for the words, they are simply a way to focus my intent, much the same way you would say something out loud to help you remember."

"How about—" Cullen suddenly stopped talking when he realized they were no longer alone. Fiana had strolled casually into their grove. Into his dream!

"Sorry to interrupt," she smirked. "But I thought you might want to know how to get your witch back."

"She's not a witch," Cullen flung back angrily.

"Oh, did I say witch? I meant to say bi—"

"Enough petty banter," Rowan cut in. "I suppose you have some demands?"

"Come now. Surely you could spare a few moments to flirt with an old flame." Fiana twirled her hair around a pale finger and batted her eyelashes.

"Just tell us what you want," sighed Rowan.

Fiana put on a winsome pout.

Rowan waited.

Cullen rolled his eyes.

"Very well then. I want you to meet me at the westernmost point of Deception Pass. Be there at midnight tomorrow, and I will release the teacher."

"Where is Deception Pass," asked Cullen.

"I'm not going to make it that easy for you. Do your homework. After all, you have to let me have some fun."

"You are just going to release her?" Rowan asked.

"Of course. She's of no use to me anymore," she said with a smile.

"Why should we believe you?" Cullen asked, scowling.

"Just be there," was the condescending reply right before she vanished.

Cullen turned toward Rowan. "We can't trust her," he said.

"I agree," Rowan replied. "She means to trade the teacher for me. Which will kill you. We must come up with an alternative plan. You must also tell the others what we've learned.

Max knew someone was watching her. She could feel their eyes upon her. It was a decidedly uncomfortable sensation, so it brought her meditations to an end. She opened her eyes.

The face of a man peered in at her through the barred window. It was a dark face of late middle-age, worn by the elements and hard living. A touch of madness peered through his focused gaze, and his snaggle-toothed grin was more than unsettling.

Surprised, she found that it didn't inspire fear within her but stirred up a mixture of pity and revulsion. She didn't sense any danger or ill intent from him, but she did feel relief that there was a wall between them.

"Who are you?" she asked.

The man shuffled his feet nervously before replying almost shyly.

"Caleb."

After speaking his name, he stopped moving and began looking around in a quite bizarre manner. Then his gaze lolled back to her, and he held it there with rapt attention.

Max tried again. "What are you doing here?"

He started shuffling his feet again, added a shrug, and then answered, "I live here."

"Do you work for Fiana?"

Bitterness twisted his features. He turned his head and spat. "She's evil. I do nothing for her. Defiance is all she deserves."

Well. That's a relief, she thought. *My enemy's enemy and all that. Now for the million-dollar question:* "Can you help me get out of here?"

"Oh now, I couldn't do that!"

Her hopes deflated.

"Why not?"

"The Spirit Mother has forbidden it. I would help you if I could. You are so beautiful. So very, very beautiful." He reached a dirty hand through the bars to touch Max's face, but she recoiled as a reflex. Ashamed, he pulled his hand back in close and looked at the ground.

Max felt bad about reacting so. On top of that, she was confused and frustrated. Nevertheless, she persevered. This Caleb seemed to be her best hope, if not for escape then at least for information.

"Who is this Spirit Mother?" she asked.

"She is who I serve. She looks after me, takes care of me. Helps me when she can. She is powerful, but she was tricked, trapped and enslaved. Now she must do as the evil one commands."

"You don't do as the evil one says?"

"Oh no! She is bad bad bad. I defy her," he said, spitting again. "I would free my mistress if I could. I will when I find out how. Well, I know how, but I can't get to her. She's kept locked up behind glass in the mansion. And the house is guarded by the evil one's people. I can't get in to help my mistress." His spoken thoughts took a sharp turn. "They are all asleep now, so I came down here to look at you. You are so beautiful. So very beautiful." He reached his hand through the bars again, but this time Max forced herself not to recoil. His hand touched her cheek; it was clammy and dirty, and it smelled bad. Max suppressed a shudder and wondered if she would feel any safer outside the cell with this unsettling man. She backed away when he didn't stop stroking her cheek on his own. He smiled at her. It was both lewd and innocent at the same time. What a strange, disturbing man.

"Do you ever leave the island?" Max asked, trying to get his mind off her.

"No, never. It is my home."

"I see. How many other people live on the island?"

"Just me. And now you. Oh yes, and the girl. The evil one and and her servants are here, too, but they are asleep during the day. At night, I hide from them."

"And your Spirit Mother?"

"Yes, she is here, too, but she is unseen. Invisible."

Great. Ugly and crazy. Of course, stranger things have happened. After all, she was prisoner on an island inhabited by vampires and in love with a fourteen-hundred-year-old wizard. So, perhaps an invisible Spirit Mother wasn't that far fetched.

"How do you know where she is?"

"She told me."

"Does she talk to you?"

"Sometimes, when the evil one is away. She tells me she's trapped in a talisman behind glass in the mansion. We have to break the talisman to release her."

"She's not a human then?"

"Oh no! She is a Spirit!"

"Ok then."

Caleb's steady gaze was beginning to unnerve her, making her feel icky. She was also hungry and thirsty and still cold. They hadn't brought her food or water yet. She decided to try and send this disturbing visitor away if she could.

"Would you get me some food and perhaps some water and a blanket?" she asked.

He smiled with sudden joy. "Yes! That I can do! I will be back soon with food and water, and I will find something to keep you warm, too. But they cannot see it. When they come, you must hide them. Okay?"

"Okay."

He turned and bounded away quickly.

"Thank you," she called out after him, then sat down with her back to the wall and hugged her legs close, trying to retain what little heat her body produced in the chill.

CHAPTER TWENTY-ONE

The powers of Moody rivaled Rowan's, but in a different way. Money talks, as they say. With a few phone calls, he chartered a helicopter to take them all on a private tour of a lonely island off the coast of Washington. None of them had ever flown in a helicopter before, so it was very exciting, even under the circumstances. Fear dampened their enjoyment of the experience however. They didn't really know what they would encounter when they arrived and silently doubted their abilities to handle it. They had prepared as well as their imaginations allowed, but Cullen at least felt that what they would need most was something no one thought to bring. He wasn't sure what that was yet.

Ralph sat in front with the pilot. He had a gym bag full of his electronic toys at his feet. A notebook computer was open on his lap showing a fluctuating wave signal.

Mark, the pilot, had been given a story about scientific research, but he still looked dubious about the kids and the modified Boba Fett helmet Ralph wore.

Moody sat in the rear with the kids. Piled around their feet were backpacks and gym bags containing wooden stakes, crosses, and super soakers filled with holy water. Maddy and

April brought these. While April spent some time talking to Father Timmons about why a benevolent God would blind an innocent girl, Maddy had drained the holy water and refilled the basin with distilled water. It was the best she could do as a witch-in-training, but she did ask the goddess to bless it.

Their plan was to reconnoiter the island while Fiana was away, ostensibly meeting Rowan at Deception Pass, and if it seemed at all possible, find and rescue Max. They knew the island would probably be guarded by some of Fiana's vampire minions, so they wanted to be prepared, even though they expected to rely on Moody's magic primarily and were counting on Rowan to appear in a real pinch. Rowan couldn't come out before that, or Fiana would know the others were with him. The down side of this whole plan was that it had to take place after nightfall, since that was the time Fiana had specified for the meeting.

What kind of idiot goes after vampires at night? thought Cullen. He fingered the cross around his neck, wishing he had a crossbow or better yet a flame thrower or rocket launcher.

It was too loud for conversation during the flight, so they all sat alone in the darkness, ruminating in their separate fears. Cullen could see the fear on Maddy and April's faces. Even Moody looked a little worried. Mr. Ferguson was too busy on his computer to look scared or anything other than intensely focused.

Finally, their destination approached. Their nervousness increased. They had some experience with this sort of thing, after all, there was the incident in San Francisco, but only enough experience to make them realize how scared they should be.

Ralph felt particularly alone. He had never done this sort of thing before and felt apart from the group, especially since he was dealing with his fear alone. There was no one for him to talk out his anxieties with. There was no one to reach out and give his hand a squeeze as the fear continued to build. Nevertheless, he was as determined as any of them to see this through, despite his natural timidness. Concentrating on his job helped. As he studied his instruments and guided the pilot, he pushed his fears behind his science.

The spirit whom Fiana called Ariel watched the approaching craft from her confinement with mistrust. These were invaders and must have their efforts frustrated, but they were also potential new members for her tribe. Conflicting aims often troubled her since her enslavement. Working around them created difficulties at times, yet she usually managed. Her enslavement was onerous but had to be endured. Commands must be followed.

"It looks peaceful," Maddy commented in a shout over the rotating airfoils.

"Maybe everyone's gone," April shouted back.

"Don't count on it," boomed Moody. "See the house on the hill? There are lights on. Someone is home."

Ralph had turned in his seat to shout back. "Fiana at least is gone." He wore a pair of strange, lopsided glasses. They weren't his normal pair, but rather the right one had a really, really thick lens with little arms on the side of it that moved. Each arm had what looked like a tiny magnifying glass on it. He continued, "Her signature is near the main coast, but I am picking up something very strange. Something unexpected." He looked back down at his computer and started typing quickly.

"What do you mean strange?" Cullen asked, now even more nervous that he had been.

"Well, I'm not sure exactly," Ralph called back while tweaking the hand-held gadget now. "It's an unexpected anomaly in the electrical energy of the island. I've never seen anything like it," Ralph said, looking up from his gadgets momentarily, peering at them all through his weird glasses with his Boba Fett helmet comically cocked to one side.

Inside the chopper, everyone was stunned into silence as a very visible electric charge ran through all the electronics. After a very brief light display, everything shorted out.

The engine coughed a few times and died.

The rotors began to slow.

All the passengers stared at each other with fear radiating from their expressions.

The pilot cursed and fought the controls.

Their flight was turning into a plummet.

Moody suddenly roused himself and began barking rapid commends in Gaelic. The night sky rushed by far too quickly. The tree tops leapt towards them. Everyone found something to desperately cling to.

Then their plummet slowed to a fall. Some control returned to their decent. Somehow, between Moody's efforts and the pilot's, they managed a precipitous but safe landing, which rattled their teeth but did no real harm.

As the blades slowly spun to a stop, everyone sat staring into the darkness, silent except for their heavy breathing. Finally, the pilot turned to Moody and asked very deliberately, "What's going on!"

After a few more deep breaths, Moody casually replied, "Obviously your vehicle is in need of some maintenance, my good man. Why don't you see what you can do about it while we go see if we can find some help here. We saw a house on the way in, so we'll start there."

The pilot stared for a moment longer without expression before nodding once and saying, "Right."

Feeling that the bird was no longer in friendly territory, the whole gang quickly gathered their gear and tumbled out into the North Pacific night. After moving a cautious distance away, they gathered together for comfort and looked apprehensively into the darkness.

Maddy and April armed themselves with the super soakers. They put the stakes in the back pockets of their jeans for easy access. They handed out all the crosses, and each of their party put them obediently on, except Cullen, who already wore his.

"What do we do now?" asked Ralph, trying to get the cross over his Boba Fett helmet.

Well said, thought Cullen, *What now?*

"I guess we explore," hazarded Maddy.

"There's someone out there," said April. "I can see them."

"Where?" asked Moody.

"How can anyone see anything in this blackness?" asked Ralph.

"At the moment, she can see better than any of us," said Cullen.

"Off to the left and forward about two dozen yards," said April, ignoring the peanut gallery.

Moody spoke a single word, "*Solas.*" Commanding, yet weary, as if reaching his limit. A faint glow lit up the area April had indicated, revealing a large tree and beneath it a bent figure, startled by his sudden exposure, began hobbling away.

"Wait!" called April. "Who are you?"

The figure hesitated and turned back towards them.

"No light," he hissed in a quavery voice. "It's not safe."

"Come here then," said Moody, banishing the glow with a gesture, as the old man cautiously approached. "Who are you?"

"I am Caleb," he said. "I live here, but others live here now too, and they are evil."

"We know," said April.

"They have taken a friend of ours, and we need to rescue her," Moody offered.

"The beautiful lady, yes I know of her. So beautiful."

"Do you know where she is?" Ralph asked eagerly, stepping in front of the others.

Caleb regarded his strange appearance from head to toe for a moment before continuing, "They've hidden her underground, but I know where. I found her. She was kind to me. I promised to help."

"Will you take us to her?"

"Yes, I can do that, but we must hurry. We shouldn't linger in the open. Evil things are out at night. Evil things that play cruel games with innocent people."

"Lead on MacDuff," said Ralph.

Caleb seemed to have no difficulty making his way through the dark landscape, but the others were less sure-footed. Among them, only April seemed to have little trouble, so Maddy held on to April's elbow for a change. The others did the best they could, stumbling along in single file.

It was a beautiful night. Gusts of wind brought the scents of the sea to awaken their olfactory senses while making the stunted pines wave their limbs about in celebration. Adrenaline kept them all keyed up, more awake and aware of their surroundings than they would be otherwise. They were somehow able to appreciate the world around them, despite constantly searching it for dangers.

They made their way toward the water where a large section of cliff jutted into the crashing waves like a stone prow. The crashing sounds of the waves beating against the rock was tremendous, assaulting their senses with their primal force. This was not a safe place.

Caleb led them down a stony staircase, and Cullen thought that they were putting way too much trust into this strange man. Many caves yawned in the cliff face below, carved by millennia of waves eating away at the softer material. As they reached the end of the staircase, Caleb led them into one of these openings.

Complete darkness filled the interior.

"Down there, behind a locked door. She cannot get out." Caleb indicated the crevice further inside the cave, but remained at the mouth of the cave himself.

"We'll get her out," said Ralph, determined. He started moving deeper into the darkness.

"She's not in there," said Maddy.

Ralph stopped and turned back.

"What's that you say child?" asked Moody, placing a hand on her shoulder.

"She isn't down there. Caleb is planning to betray us. I can feel his intention."

Everyone was staring blankly in her direction, though they could see little.

Caleb began shuffling backwards, away form the group. "She's imagining things," he wheedled. "There is no danger inside, only out here!"

"How true," said a new voice from the darkness.

"They're all around us," said April.

"Yes, and something else," said Maddy, as pieces of darkness began to coalesce into sinister shapes outside the cave.

Panic infused them all, but in Cullen it took a different form. He felt himself losing control and Rowan struggling to emerge. Darkness was engulfing him.

Ralph stood frozen with shock, as useless as Cullen felt.

The two girls began drenching their attackers with the super soakers filled with holy water. It made the vampires curse with annoyance and hang back. Although it made their skin sizzle and burn, it did little actual harm to them.

Moody was gathering what strength remained to him after his exhaustive landing of the helicopter, but events outpaced him.

Rowan burst forth with wand in hand ready to hurl magics about, only to be engulfed by power stronger than his own which held him fast.

The super soakers were running dry.

"Into the cave," yelled Moody. "I will hold the entrance."

They all ran for it while Rowan looked on helplessly, remembering a similar occurrence. He would stand and fight this time.

The power which held his magic down was a nature spirit, not evil in itself, but enslaved by a darkness he recognized as Fiana's. How had Fiana ensnared such a puissant being? If he could only free it from Fiana's control, they might have a chance. Otherwise he feared they were all lost. He abandoned his struggle to break free, trying instead to free his captor. But that proved as futile as his own release from this distance. He felt the power nearby, but it wasn't close enough. Especially since it was hindering his own magics.

The others had disappeared down into the cave. Moody summoned an effective barrier so they were safe for the moment, but also trapped inside. And Rowan was isolated on the outside of Marlin's protective force, near the mouth of the cave.

Fiana's fiends encircled him. The leather clad one plucked Rowan's wand from his grasp.

"You at least are fairly caught," James sneered. Then to his minions, "bind him and bring him to the manse."

Rowan's companions watched in horror from deep within the cave as he was dragged away.

"Cullen!" April said.

"Don't worry, lass," Moody offered, "Everything will be all right."

Ralph doubted it. Nothing was all right. They had been foolishly cornered deep inside a cave on an island inhabited by a bunch of vampires that could only be reached by helicopter. How could anything be all right?

Their best bet was to wait for morning, when the vampires were asleep, or at least, weakened. They could not see anyone or anything stirring outside the cave, but they knew there would be watchers waiting for their escape.

They had lost Cullen, and with him their most powerful ally, Rowan.

What were they to do?

Moody was exhausted.

Ralph was recriminating himself for being an ineffectual coward.

Maddy was re-living the familiar despair of being lost in darkness, only now it was far more real.

April alone felt compelled to go on, remembering what Bilbo had said in a similar situation. Cullen had made her a copy of the book on tape for her birthday last year. She spoke it aloud:

"Go back, no use. Sideways, impossible, forward, the only way, so let's get on with it."

"We don't know what's down there." Ralph objected.

"But we do know what's up here," she replied. "It is very unlikely that what is down there is worse.

"The young one is right," sighed Moody. "Let us see if there is a back door to this trap. Can anyone provide a light? I'm too weakened even for a simple spell at the moment. My apologies, friends."

"I have a laser pointer," offered Ralph pathetically. "How could I be so stupid not to bring a flashlight."

"Never mind that," said April. "It will have to do. I can see well enough, so I will lead. Come along Maddy, take hold of my elbow again. Let me lead you for a while longer. The rest of you follow behind and do the same, make a chain of yourselves behind Maddy. While there's life, there's hope, as Sam would say."

"Who is Sam?" asked Ralph.

"Sam Gamgee from *The Lord of the Rings*," said April as she tried her best to embrace the blackness of the cave. She had had many conversations with Cullen on the story in addition to the audio book, so she knew it well.

"I am afraid I have never read it," admitted Ralph.

They descended deeper into the darkness.

CHAPTER TWENTY-TWO

Daylight still lingered in her cell when Max awoke, still curled in a tight ball. Every muscle in her body ached from being tensed up against the cold of the night. Her hips felt as though nails had been driven into them from laying on the hard ground. She swore her body actually creaked like an old barn door as she stood up. She peered out of the window at the daylight outside. She saw trees, lots of trees, and water. Even more water than trees. Endless water.

Her neck felt bruised and tender. She touched it gingerly, assessing the damage. There below her old scar were the two new wounds with crispy, flaky dried blood all around it. There is no covering up all this with a scarf. She had lost a lot of blood. It was really the only explanation as to why she was able to sleep at all. She was just too weakened to do anything else. Despite her best efforts to utilize her calming techniques, this was all just too traumatic for her to remain calm. She must've passed out from the loss of blood and hunger. Caleb never had returned with food or water. The panic began to rise in her chest again, and she tried to calm herself. She closed her eyes and pictured herself in her bed at home, cuddled up under her comforter and another blanket. Safe and warm at home. When she got back there, she would never leave, never ever leave.

"Never ever leave," she said aloud.

"Yes you will," a thin voice came from nowhere.

Max's eyes popped open. "What? Who's there?"

"Aidan," the disembodied voice replied. "I'm a prisoner, too."

Max remembered Caleb saying something about a girl on the island. Perhaps this is who he had meant.

"The walls are thin between our cells," Aidan continued, "Well, relatively thin for stone. We couldn't kick them down or anything, but if we had a spoon or something we could probably dig our way through in a decade or so." She laughed. The sound of her laughter was slightly tinged with despair. "There is a small hole just here," Aidan said.

Max looked around some more, and then she saw it: a small hole with a smaller twig poking in and out of it. Max ran over to the hole.

"Aidan?"

"Yes. I'm here! It's so nice to have someone to talk to again."

"How long have you been here?"

"I don't know. A long time," Aidan replied. Her voice sounded quite young to Max's ears.

"How old are you?" Max asked.

"Well, when I was brought here, I was fifteen, but I'm not sure how long ago that was. I might be sixteen now."

Max felt very sad for the girl. She felt very scared for them both.

"Why do they keep you here, Aidan?" Max actually wanted to know why she was here alive, after all, this girl would be a tasty snack for them.

"I can do stuff," she said in a small voice.

"Do stuff? What do you mean?"

"You wouldn't believe me, but I swear it's true."

Max laughed bitterly. "I'll believe you. I've seen a lot of things over the past few months that I wouldn't have believed a year ago, but I'll believe just about anything now. Besides, we have to keep each other company, right?"

Aidan was quiet for a long time, as if she was thinking about whether or not she could trust Max. Max just waited patiently, taking mild comfort in the fact that she wasn't alone down here. Everything got very quiet. Max could hear the birds faintly singing in the sunshine. She wondered if she would ever feel the warmth of the sun on her skin again.

"I can start fires," Aidan finally said, tearing Max away from her disturbing thoughts.

"Like with matches?" Max asked. She could start fires. That wasn't strange. Anyone could start fires.

"Of course with matches!" Aidan laughed, "but without matches, too. Just by thinking about it. What's more: fire can't hurt me either. It's like I'm immune to it. I used to not be able to control it, starting the fires, that is, but I've gotten better at it. Still. I think that's why they took me. I heard them say something once about feeding on me for my power or something. Then something about an elemental." Aidan sighed. She sounded tired, resigned. "I just wish I didn't have this stupid power. It's been nothing but trouble."

Max found it difficult to believe this girl could start fires with her mind, but she wasn't going to say anything. After all, she didn't want to offend the girl. And stranger things—y'know? Her favorite student being possessed by a very handsome Druid, for example.

"What kind of trouble?" Max asked, just trying to keep the conversation going. It was nice to have someone to talk to. Especially when that someone wasn't a potentially dangerous and very creepy madman. Perhaps it would keep both their minds off their predicament.

"Well, the worst trouble was when I was a little girl. I had a bad nightmare. It was a weird dream. My Raggedy Ann doll jumped down from my headboard onto my face and started beating me. Her flimsy, rag doll arms flailing in anger against me. I was so scared! I was only nine or ten. There was some sort of spontaneous reaction and I just burst into flames. Raggedy Ann burned right up, and the ashes fell all over me. But I thought it was all in the dream. I woke up screaming from the assault, and I was on fire! Only it didn't burn me. It was just burning my bed and everything else. There was fire all around me.

"My mother ran into the bedroom and scooped up my little brother to carrying him out. My father was trying to get me, but I wouldn't go. I thought I was still dreaming. Then he caught on fire. It was horrible. I tried to wake up but I couldn't. I didn't realize it was no longer a dream until it was too late. He died trying to save me. He wouldn't give up until he could save me. He died because of me. I ran away. I couldn't deal. I don't know if my mother and brother made it out alive or not, but I couldn't face them having killed my father. I probably killed them all. I just ran and ran because I didn't know what else to do. I sat under a stone bridge until I stopped flaming. That's what I call it when it happens: flaming."

There was another burst of hysterical laughter.

"Like the human torch. Flame on, sister!" Bitterness this time.

"That sounds horrible," Max said.

"Tell me about it. The guilt alone probably should have killed me, but, what do they call it? Survival instinct. That's it. I guess that kicked in. Or something. Whatever."

"What did you do then? How did you survive?"

"Lots of things I really don't want to talk about. But I was eventually taken in by a circus magician who raised me somewhat. Trained me also. Helped me control my power, as he called it. Some power. I sure wouldn't be here without it, and I'd still have a family..." Her voice faded off and Max felt her turn away from the tiny chink in the wall.

"Aidan?"

No answer.

"Aidan?"

All Max could hear now was the wind in the trees, or was it Aidan crying?

"Okay. Maybe we can talk again later. I'll tell you my story, although it's not..." Max didn't know what to say. "I'll be around," Max managed, "You know, if you want to talk some more. We can talk about other things." She tried to keep a smile in her voice, but she had a feeling that she failed miserably.

Power.

They were keeping the girl to feed on her power.

Maybe that's why they didn't kill her, Max, too. She couldn't start fires or anything like that, but she did have Fey blood in her veins. Probably like a drug to them.

CHAPTER TWENTY-THREE

"Hey," exclaimed April, "There are stairs here leading up. Maybe it is a way out."

"Yeah," replied Maddy dryly, "because that's just our luck."

"Oh, come on! Let's at least give it a try!"

Always the optimist.

"Might as well. It's not like we have anything better to do," Maddy admitted.

"We could just sit here and bitch and moan," April said sarcastically.

"Meow," said Maddy.

April laughed.

"Hey, I'm a multi-tasker," Maddy played along. "I can bitch and moan and climb stairs at the same time. Just don't expect me to chew gum, too."

Despite themselves, the girls couldn't help giggling just a little. It helped with the nervous tension but caused Ralph to grit his teeth.

"Up it is then," said Moody. "We shall ascend to a higher place."

"Physically, if not intellectually," muttered Ralph under his breath. But if he was heard by the others, they didn't acknowledge the taunt.

They climbed. After about three hundred steps, they paused to catch their breath. Moody sat down, panting.

"I fear I am in danger of losing some girth!" he said breathlessly.

"Hush," admonished Maddy in a whisper. "There is something close."

Everyone tried to hold their breath at the same time they were trying to catch it.

"I think there are guards at the top of the stairs," she hissed in a whisper.

"What do we do?" asked Ralph.

"Go back down?" whispered April.

Moody groaned softly.

"We need to make a plan," insisted Ralph. "We can't do that here."

"I think we can if we keep it down," Maddy contradicted. "They aren't close enough to hear us. I can barely sense them myself. They're around a couple of bends and maybe a thousand steps up."

Moody groaned again, a little louder than before.

"I have an idea that might work," offered Ralph. "It will take some time to set up, and probably some cunning as well."

With James fiercely gripping his left arm and another minion his right, Rowan was hauled into a large chamber where Fiana was pacing furiously. Husband and wife were once again face to face. Three months after the first time they had seen each other in fourteen centuries, for Fiana anyway. In Rowan's mind those fourteen hundred years passed in a few moments, only to discover that all he knew was gone and his wife had become a vampire. Actually, an evil vampire with a goddess complex.

The last time they had met, she had tortured him and tried to turn him as well. After he escaped and convinced her to go merrily into the Otherworld where she belonged, she tricked him at the last minute with a kiss and escaped. Now they were all in the same room again. The tension was so thick, one couldn't even cut it with a knife. One would at least need a hammer and chisel. Maybe a jackhammer.

"Hello, my love," Fiana sneered. "So nice to see you again."

"Cut the pleasantries. I know what you are now, woman. I will not be fooled again by sentimentalities." Rowan's eyes glowed with angry fire as he looked at his once-beloved.

"Oh my, my! You make me shiver! But then, you always did." She pursed her lips, batted her eyes, and threw a quiet, spontaneous spell at him, but Rowan's reflexes were too quick. With a sudden twist of his body, he jerked James around in front of him as a shield. James crumpled to the floor in agony as he was hit by Fiana's spell. Rowan had snatched his wand from the now-limp hand as James had fallen to the ground. The other minion let go of Rowan and prudently backed away.

Rowan, poised to strike back, said, "Like I said. I will not be caught off guard by you again. You cannot trick me with your wiles again, woman."

Fiana smiled warmly, and for a moment Rowan felt his resolve falter. But only for a moment. Perhaps he had spoken too soon. She was still so beautiful, but sentimentality would not only get him killed, Max and the girls would be killed, too. And Cullen. He must protect Cullen no matter what. After all, he was just a child, just a boy. He had stumbled into this mess which should have ended fourteen centuries ago.

What, after all, had all their efforts accomplished?

Their tribe who they had been meant to protect was no more. Their people may have survived the attack, but no children were ever born to those survivors. And what children there were just went on as children. Forever in the Otherworld.

An entire people removed from the circle of life.

Was that really what their magic was all about? The only people left to save were the ones who were alive now. He knew that Fiana would never release someone who was in her power. Still, he figured, that if he could stall for time, the others might be able to come up with something.

"If it is still what you wish, I will trade myself for the teacher, but I will not submit until you show her to me. Unharmed," Rowan said. The disgust he felt for Fiana showed all over his face. He couldn't hide his emotions well. Sometimes he felt this was one of his biggest faults, but usually, he counted it as a blessing.

"She's fine, my sweet, trust me," Fiana toyed with him. She twirled her thin, ivy-carved wand between her slender fingers, smiling at him while she did so.

This infuriated Rowan ever further. Her ability to keep her cool made the angry fire within him rise again. He must control his anger, or she would catch him off guard.

"And the boy," Rowan said, containing his anger, "do you promise he will be safe?"

"Of course," Fiana said.

"We tried to separate, but we could not. How will you be able to separate us?"

"Trust me," she repeated.

"I will never trust you again, woman," Rowan flared.

Fiana faked a pout, pushing her bottom lip out and bowing her head, but delight shone from her green eyes. She batted them innocently at Rowan.

Rowan grasped his wand tightly. The veins in his forehead and arms protruded with his anger. His face crimsoned. He still found her total transformation so hard to believe, and it made him angrier than ever. "There is no deal if the boy is hurt."

"The boy will feel no pain," Fiana said. "I promise. He will feel nothing." Total seriousness covered the features of her face.

Rowan nodded in agreement. He saw through her deception but pretended otherwise.

"Now come to me, my love. Come to me of your own accord and kiss me, or rather, let me *kiss* you."

Rowan looked over his shoulder and wondered what was happening with the others. He must stall further. Give them time to escape. He couldn't count on a rescue. But if he kept Fiana busy, maybe they could get away.

He watched for his own opportunity.

As soon as he thought it, he cursed himself. Was she in his mind? Looking back at Fiana quickly, he tried to see in her features if she knew what he was thinking, if she had heard his thought. But Fiana's face hadn't changed one bit. She was either a master of deceit, or she did not know his plan.

"Like I said, woman, I want to see Maxine alive and well first."

Fiana smiled slightly. Only one corner of her mouth turned up. "Very well." She clapped her hands twice.

James, who had by this time recovered enough to drag himself to his feet exited the room through a door behind Fiana.

"I can't understand what you see in that one," Fiana remarked. "Sure there is a little power there, but hardly in our league."

"Have you truly forgotten so much? Once we stood together and fought against people like you've become."

For an instant, Fiana actually looked perturbed, but she recovered quickly enough to maintain deniability.

"I have gained wisdom over the years, while you remain a fool."

"Perhaps in your wisdom you have forgotten that in all the old tales the fool succeeds where the heroes fail."

Fiana smiled maliciously. "Not in this one, my love."

"This tale is not yet sung."

"Maybe not, but it will be my bard who sings it."

James re-entered the room holding Max lasciviously close and licking his lips, which were covered in what Rowan could only assume to be her blood.

"I said unharmed!" Rowan squeezed out through clenched teeth, shooting a hateful glance to Fiana.

"Oh, that's just a scratch, my love. She will be just fine," Fiana said.

Another door opened, and in came Moody, April, and Maddy, all held by other vampires, baring their fangs.

"They, on the other hand, will not be just fine."

CHAPTER TWENTY-FOUR

Rowan's confidence plummeted when he saw the captives but maintained some hope when he realized that Ralph was still at large.

"So," observed Fiana, "was this the rescue party you were counting on? Was your surrender just stalling? Did you actually think this pathetic gaggle would save you?" she said with derisive laughter.

"What about our deal," he asked, already knowing the answer.

She was no longer laughing and her eyes turned black.

"You had no intention of releasing Max in exchange for me. Do you think I am completely daft, woman? You are not the woman I married. You have proven that more than once now."

"And what was your great plan, Rowan? Hmmm?" She started towards him with deliberate strides. "I am far more powerful than you. You are on my turf surrounded by my minions. What is your grand plan for escape, Rowan?"

Rowan's nostrils flared as she looked into his eyes, close enough to kiss him. He had a brief flash of his wedding day, which still remained so fresh in his mind. How they kissed and laughed. How happy they felt for those few mintues after they were wed, before the raiders came. A happy moment that has been lost to antiquity. He remembered the joy of kissing her and holding her. How blissful it had been just to be near her. He hated himself for the rash decision that had led them all to this moment.

"You are right, of course," Fiana grinned. She traced his lips with her finger, tilting her head up to him. Her eyes remained black, but her face had softened.

She was a master of deceit after all.

"You made a foolish choice then, and you've made a foolish choice today. Nice to know some things never change."

Rowan pushed her forcibly back and put some distance between them.

Fiana laughed, and her eyes returned to their captivating green.

"You never had any intention of releasing Max," Rowan confirmed.

"That's true."

"And the boy would have been destroyed," he continued.

"Also true, but with this little stunt, my love, not only will the teacher and the boy die, so will these three," she said the last with a bit of contempt and a flick of her wand in their general direction.

Rowan knew she wasn't bluffing. His naïvety would be the death of them all.

"You don't have us all," Maddy said defiantly, holding her head up proudly, although she was held back by a vampire.

"Hush, you foolish girl," Moody said crossly.

"No! I'm not going to die here tonight," she said, looking Moody square in the eyes. She turned back to Fiana. "I'll make you a deal. There are more of us, one who also loves the teacher," she said, indicating Max. "He's still out there. It must hurt you to know that two men here care for this teacher more than they care for you. Make that three," she said, looking back at Moody again.

"Maddy?" April said as a tear fell down her face.

Maddy ignored the horror and betrayal displayed on April's face. "Shut up. I won't be *pwned* by this horrid witch. Give me your word that you'll let me go, and I'll tell you the entire plan."

"So there actually is a plan? I'm surprised. What is it? Who else is out there?" Fiana was amused and curious.

"Who else? Who else is here?" Max asked.

James held her tighter and licked up the side of her neck.

Max grimaced.

"Mr. Ferguson," Maddy said.

"Ralph," Max said with a hint of longing and regret in her voice.

"Enough of this. Tell me where he is now, child. What is he planning and who else is with him? I don't have time for your games," Fiana said.

"Swear you'll let me live," Maddy insisted.

"How about I'll kill you quickly if you tell me, or the pain will start now if you don't," Fiana said, walking more closely to Maddy. She was fiddling with her wand, pressing one end of it into one palm with the other, then twirling it around nimbly between her long, white fingers.

"Um..." Maddy said, inching back. She seemed to lose some confidence, like perhaps her plan had backfired.

"Lady," Moody said, taking Fiana's attention away from Maddy. "Show mercy. If not for us, then at least for yourself. I have known you to be quite merciful. Just let us go. You have your husband back. These girls have done you no harm."

Fiana regarded him for a moment.

"I remember telling you that I would kill you if I ever saw your face again," she said to Moody, who in turn looked rather hurt. "I was in no position to do that last November, but I am in such a position now."

She was toying with him.

"Think me not a woman of my word? You of all people should know, Moody, that I'm true to my word." She looked over to Rowan, who stood alone, helpless. He knew that if he tried anything, they would all die. "Well, most of the time," she added with a smile. "Still, what you say is true. Almost true; but these children would be so very tasty. I do love an innocent's blood, so sweet and pure."

Maddy laughed. More a snort than a laugh.

"Oh yes, I suppose you are not as innocent as you...look," Fiana said with a scowl, waving her hand around, indicating Maddy's unique outfit.

"That one likes blood play," James said. He still held Max uncomfortably close. Fiana's other minions smiled and snickered behind him.

"So I see," Fiana said. She touched her wand to the arm coverings that extended to Maddy's elbow. Maddy tried to pull back, but she could not. Fiana yanked one down and revealed the angry, red cuts beneath them.

Maddy's eyes filled with tears and hatred.

"Leave her alone!" April said.

"Perhaps we'll turn this one, too," Fiana said to James. "We have room for another female, and this one is so deliciously dark already. She'll make a good servant. I could always use another servant."

"I'll never serve you," Maddy said through tears, partially of embarrassment and partially of anger.

"Oh, but you won't have a choice, my dear," Fiana said. Her lips still smiled, but her eyes looked tired. "Kill them all," she said with a wave of her hand.

"No!" Max, Moody, and Rowan shouted all at once.

Rowan leapt forward, his wand at the ready. "*Stadiam*," he shouted, pointing the wand at the vampire that held both girls.

Fiana blocked his spell with a lazy flick of her wrist.

"Really, my love? Surely you realize that you're out numbered."

The vampire holding the girls hadn't moved, as if he was waiting to see what the magic would do to him.

"I said kill them, you fool," Fiana said angrily whipping her head back over her shoulder, but she didn't turn to face them. She kept her eye on Rowan. He was that hero type, and he would surely try something else.

The vampire suddenly let go of both the girls. The vampire holding Moody let go as well, and James jumped back from Max at the exact same time, both with shrieks of pain.

"Quickly now!" Moody said, and they all rushed together.

Fiana now turned from Rowan to see about the commotion behind her. It wasn't the screams and begging she had expected, and so grown to love.

"He burned us, my lady," James offered. "The fat one. I told you you should've gotten rid of him back in New York."

"Silence!" Fiana said to James. She turned to Moody. "Although, he might be right. I have learned time and again that mercy leads to problems. Well, better late than never." She waved her wand in a grand motion and pointed it intensely at Moody, but nothing happened. Rowan had pointed his wand at her to stop her from hurting any of them, shouting "*Stadiam*" again, but nothing resulted from his efforts either.

They both looked at their wands as if they were broken.

Fiana shook hers next to her ear as if listening for a rattling inside to indicate that it was indeed broken.

The door behind her opened up and Ralph walked in.

"I hope I'm not too late," Ralph said.

"Ralph," Max cried in joy, happy to see him. Surprised at just how happy she was to see him.

"You are just on time, my good man. Just on time," Moody said, who had been holding the girls close to him for protection.

Moody, April, and Maddy all rushed behind Ralph who stood with his modified Boba Fett helmet on his head and more gadgets in his hands. He was pointing something toward them all that looked remarkably like an old cell phone. Max, now free of James's grasp, rushed towards Ralph, who held open his arms to receive her. He held her close with one arm while holding the other steady with the cell-phone-thingy.

"Thanks for stalling, kid," Ralph said to Maddy.

"No problem, now let's get out of here."

"What? You can't just leave!" Fiana said incredulously. She is not defied. Not ever!

"Watch us," Maddy snapped, readjusting her arm coverings.

Rowan walked over to his friends.

"No!" Fiana screamed, and she tried to use her wand again.

"I've blocked the magic," Ralph said proudly. "There is no use in trying."

"But how—" Fiana stumbled.

"Physics, of course. I disrupted the energy surrounding you and Rowan, and it interrupts what you call magic. What you call magic, I call physics."

CHAPTER TWENTY-FOUR

"Who are you, Einstein?" Fiana sneered.

"Hawking would be closer."

"You may have blocked our magic, but you forget, magic is just a convenience. We do still have supernatural strength, and without magic, you all are now more vulnerable than ever."

Fiana smiled once again when she saw their confidence falter.

"Boys," Fiana said, gesturing to the vampires behind her. They all growled and moved ahead.

CHAPTER TWENTY-FIVE

The would-be rescuers huddled closer together. Ralph still held Max close and protectively with one arm, but the hand that held his scrambling cell-phone-looking gadget-thingy began to tremble.

Moody held the girls tightly on each side of his massive belly.

Rowan stood alone with his wand at the ready out of habit.

"Now what?" whispered Ralph out of the side of his mouth.

Stalling again, Maddy ripped off the cross from around her neck and said, "Catch," throwing the cross to Fiana who instinctively caught it.

Nothing happened.

Fiana laughed. "I'm not a Christian," she said, tossing the cross behind over her shoulder.

James caught it before he knew what he was doing. It seared his hands and he yelped in pain. The entire room filled with the scent of burned flesh.

"Um—does anyone have a stake?" asked Moody.

The vampires had taken the wooden stakes away from Maddy and April. The super soakers were empty and, let's face it, pretty ineffective.

"Wait," April said smiling, "We have something better."

"Yes!" Maddy said smiling with her.

The doors behind Fiana blew open, and a gush of white wind came flowing in.

"Ariel!" Fiana said.

"Who is Ariel," asked Ralph.

"She is the resident spirit of the island," explained Moody. "The one who damaged our flying machine."

The white wind took the smoky form of a beautiful woman which hovered in the air above them all. She stood between the vampires and the others and extended her smoky arms out to the side in a protective and holy stance. "You have kept me a prisoner long enough, evil one. It is time for you to leave my island, never to return."

"*Your* island?" Fiana said indignantly.

A wind funnel appeared around Fiana, sucked her off the floor, and threw her against the wall. She fell to the floor, dropping her ivy-carved wand.

"I have been here far longer than even you have been dead. Your initial spells may have caught me unaware and held me down, but I am a goddess, whereas you only pretend to be. My magic is divine power, and you can stifle it no longer. Especially now, when I have so many new believers."

"What is going on?" asked Ralph.

"One of Fiana's evils has come back to kick her in the butt," proclaimed Maddy. "I think we better get out of here while we still can."

"What about them?" Ralph asked, indicating the group of vampires who were hesitating in confusion at the unexpected defection of Ariel.

Fiana struggled, pushing herself against the wall for support and returned to her feet.

The Ariel whirlwind engulfed her again and threw her crashing into her minions. Fiana's hurled form knocked them all over like bowling pins.

"How can we thank you?" Max said to Ariel.

"You owe me nothing. By interrupting her magic, you have allowed me to be free again. So go, I will deal with these creatures."

"Time to go," declared Moody, and they all rushed for the exit, leaping over the struggling pile of undead bodies between them and the door.

"Thank you, Ariel," April called back.

The beautiful, melodic voice of Ariel followed them out. "It is I who have been blessed by you."

Horrifying screams from inside the castle house followed, and the group ran faster.

CHAPTER TWENTY-SIX

"Wait!" Max cried as they ran from the mansion. "We have to get Aidan. She's still trapped in the cell by the sea."

"Who?" asked Maddy.

"Aidan. She's a girl. They have her captive in the dungeon, too."

"Do you know how to get to her?" asked Rowan.

"Uh-oh," said Ralph, shaking the cell-phone-looking gadget in his hand.

"No," Max said, "but I bet he does." She pointed to Caleb's hunched form peering around a tree to look upon the distant chaos.

"What do you mean 'Uh-oh'?" demanded Maddy.

"Um, this jammer draws a lot of current, and the batteries are about to die. We don't have much more time."

Caleb tried to creep away, but Rowan acted swiftly. Caleb only had time to squeal in alarm before a strong tattoo-covered hand grasped him firmly around the back of his neck. Rowan steered him forcibly toward the rest of the group.

"You might as well turn it off," April suggested to Ralph, who was still shaking his gadget as if it would extend the battery life. "Fiana has her hands full with Ariel, and we may need Rowan's magic before this is all over."

Max went over to Caleb, who was trembling and cowering in panic. "Calm down. We won't hurt you. We just need you to take us to Aidan. Can you do that?"

Caleb nodded with evident fear.

"And no leading us into a trap this time," added Maddy, pointing a very angry finger right against his nose.

"I only wanted to keep the beautiful lady for myself," Caleb whined. "I'm so alone on this island," he sobbed.

Max shuddered.

"And no whining," added April.

Rowan released his neck but kept a firm grip in his collar.

"This way," muttered Caleb as he proceeded to lead them towards the caves.

Before too long they stood before a stone door. A single slab of rock had been bolted to the cave wall with massive iron hinges.

"Wouldn't a wooden door work just as well?" asked Maddy.

"Aidan is a fire raiser," explained Max. "Nothing that wasn't fire proof could hold her."

"An elemental," said Rowan. "Truly rare beings." Rowan touched his wand to the door and said a single word: *"Fosgail."* It obediently swung open. Behind it, a girl of sixteen-ish stood blinking at them in confusion.

A desperate gurgle issued from Rowan's throat as if words were struggling to get out. He collapsed to the floor and a moment later Cullen, on hands and knees, looked up at Aidan and whispered hoarsely, "I thought you were dead."

"Oh Cullen!" Aidan cried and ran to him, dropping to her knees so she could wrap her arms around him.

"Okay," said Maddy.

Everyone else just stared with confused astonishment. Silent tears slid down the faces of Cullen and Aidan, still embracing.

"The fire," Max said, understanding. "Oh, how wonderful!"

They all looked from Cullen and Aidan to Max, whom they regarded with even more confusion.

Finally, it was Ralph who spoke. "Uh—I'm not sure what's going on, but we still need to get out of here."

"Quite right," agreed Moody as he moved to gently help the two to their feet.

"She's my sister," Cullen explained. "I thought she died in the fire with my father."

"Oh Cullen," was all Aidan could say and cried harder.

When they got outside Aidan's former cell, they could see the lights of their helicopter making its way back towards the mainland.

"He left without us! That jerk!" Maddy exclaimed.

"Well," said April, "I don't really suppose we can blame him."

"Well I'm going to anyway," Maddy declared, folding her arms angrily across her chest.

"Come on," said Max. "We'll take her boat." She led them down towards the dock.

Caleb slunk back.

"All right," April said. "Stay if you want, but you're welcome to come with us."

"Where would I go? What would I do? This island is all I know." He shrugged and looked down. "Now my goddess is free from the evil ones. It will be just she and I now, like it's supposed to be."

The others said their goodbyes and went to the boat, relieved for the most part.

Caleb crept back to wherever he called home.

Dawn was just beginning to break, and there was a long journey ahead. There were several boats at the dock, so they chose a small luxury yacht, since they would spend an entire day on the ocean, leisurely plowing the waves without any concerns that really mattered to them. Plus, it was equipped with the satellite phone, and there was much business to do.

Both Max and Ralph called in sick to work. Then they found a private spot to talk together for awhile in hushed tones.

Moody put in a call to the Samuels and had a financial discussion with Trudy. Upon hearing Moody's incredibly generous offer, an audible 'WOOHOO' screamed from the other end of the phone. Moody jerked the phone away from his ear and smiled at Aidan and Cullen. The new arrangement was this: for a modest six-figure sum, the Samuels would officially retain custody of Cullen, but he would live with Moody except when the social worker made her bi-annual visit.

Cullen hoped that Trudy would kick out her cheating, no-good husband and take a trip to Paris.

Which is exactly what she planned to do.

April and Maddy's mothers thought they were spending the night at the other's house, so they were unworried.

Aidan would also be staying with Moody, but no one needed to be called about that. She and Cullen didn't let go of the other's hand for the entire trip home. They talked and talked. After all, they had six years worth of catching up to do.

Cullen felt able to breath freely for the first time in years. He had family again. Plus, if he could get away from the Samuels, being possessed by a wizard was only a minor inconvenience.

"Thanks," a deep voice said inside his head.

The future looked bright all around.

na deireadh

Author's Note

The Tehwon and Winnau people are fictional tribes loosely based on several California Indian tribes. The attack on Wesh-et-wah's people during their Cirle of Life celebration is based on an actual historical event that took place in 1860. The natives who found the wand in Alaska and carried down to the redwood forest is part of this fantasy world and has no historical basis.

During the 1918 New York flu epidemic, when Fiana finds and turns James in the confines of this book, there were actual cases of people being buried alive.

The description of the holy relics during Fiana's time in 15th century England are also historically accurate, as is the story of the "True Cross."

We enjoy taking tidbits from history and incorporating them into our fantasy world. I particularly enjoy urban fantasy, as if there is magic around every corner if you just know where to look. By using some historical references, it helps make our world more real to us and to our readers.

There will be more such historical tidbits in subsequent books, as we continue to explore Fiana's path and the wand's path through history and around the globe.

Acknowledgements

The authors would like to thank...

Sharon Kirkpatrick and Nicole Hicks, along with her Beta Reading Group, for all the invaluable feedback during the editing phase.

Linda & Halla Thune for their stellar editing services. You ladies helped make this book better!

Ia Ensterä for the magnificent cover design of both *Witch on the Water* and *Rowan of the Wood*. Ia also designed the Geekalicious Gypsy Caravan, which has proven invaluable during our book tour.

Catherine Somerlot for the beautiful web design.

Jason Myers for his Adobe help.

Donna & Tom Rowe, Robert Weisheit, and Patricia & Mike Pneumatikos for their unfaltering emotional, moral, and (sometimes) financial support.

Hillary Thomas for gifting us Aidan, the elemental.

All our Twitter followers (@christinerose & @rowanofthewood), Facebook & MySpace friends, and fans around the world.
Ain't social networking grand?

ABOUT THE AUTHORS

Christine and Ethan Rose have marvelous imaginations. Often finding their inspiration among the trees, they write as they lead their lives—with plenty of adventure, magic, and love. They met swing dancing in 1999 and were married a year later. Throughout 2009, they toured the U.S. in a fancifully painted RV, affectionately called the Geekalicous Gypsy Caravan, to promote their first book *Rowan of the Wood*. They'll be continuing their adventures throughout 2010.

Although many tragic heroes begin as orphans, Ethan actually was one. Living in foster care in Sonoma County, he grew up amongst the magical redwoods in Northern California and has read virtually every fantasy novel ever written. Anglophile Christine holds her M.A. in Medieval/Renaissance Literature & Folklore. She wrote her Master's Thesis on *Le Morte D'arthur*, and produced two documentary films. She is an entrepreneur at heart and is often described as a "free spirit."

Christine's scholarly, goal-oriented background mixed with Ethan's in-depth knowledge of modern fantasy creates an impenetrable team of writers who look forward to writing many more books together. When not at home in Austin, they can be found at various Celtic Festivals and Renaissance Faires around the country with their three canine kids and Shadow, the cat, in tow.

Witch on the Water is the second novel in their *Rowan of the Wood* five-book series.

Learn more about the authors at *www.ChristineAndEthanRose.com*
Official book site & other fun stuff *www.WitchOnTheWater.com*